IMMORTAL NOX

The Lost City

Kaira Loi

Content Warning

This work contains the following topics:
graphic sex
violence
death
depression
suicidal ideation

Please be mindful of these and other possible triggers.
Seek assistance if needed from resources in your country and
practice self-care.

Chapter 1

Stretching her arms over her head, Astra swished her tail and laid her ears back with a yawn. She'd been feeling odd since getting up from an unexpected crash hours earlier. It was the first time she'd ever had that happen while playing a VR game. "Maybe it's an update?" she wondered aloud and squinted through the tree canopy at the sky's golden hue.

Tiredness was a new sensation to her while playing *Ashguard*. She'd been gathering herbs and materials for hours in-game. Long enough for the sun to begin dipping down behind the mountain range that bisected the main continent. To the north were the three major cities of Aesir, Vanaheim, and Nifelheim, and Astra Diane's current location was three months' worth of in-game travel into the unmapped Southlands.

Being a Healer Class, it was a miracle she'd made it this far by herself. Usually, she had her Porter, Xander, but she'd sent him back to Aesir to sell some things in hopes that he wouldn't catch the plague from her.

The plague plotline had come out of nowhere for a game with very little story. But attempting to find a cure for it had been a fun use of the Crafting Skills she'd spent so much time leveling up. Unfortunately, she'd caught it too, and while Players respawned at the Soul Stones in the three major cities, NPCs did not.

Astra Diane pulled her Menu out of her pocket. "I should check on him," she muttered. She hadn't been feeling the plague symptoms since her crash earlier. Her Menu, a Scroll that always existed in her pocket, was a touch screen once unrolled. Swiping through the tabs, Astra selected her teleport list.

As for the symptoms, they were miserable. It was similar to having the flu, but in her mind, the tiredness and aching in her body lingered even after logging out. Earlier that day, she'd collapsed in-game and woke up several hours later. Astra felt fine now, so she supposed the plague had run its course, and she was free to return to town.

Being in the Southlands for so long by herself was lonely. She was, after all, a squishy Healer Class and tended to rely on the fact that she could heal herself to get through fights with monsters more than an actual strategy. She knew she wasn't a very good Player.

She glanced top left to see her and Xander's health bars. The Porter was at full health, as was she. Top right, she could see the in-game time, which only showed hours and minutes of the day. That was the extent of *Ashguard's* HUD.

If she wanted to use a Skill, she had to remember and activate it. There weren't easy buttons that stayed in view to remind Players of what they had, and the Skills didn't organize into trees. A Skill simply got stronger the more it was used, and there were rumored to be hundreds of Skills out there to find. She did have a menu that listed all her Skills, but battles required quick thinking, and Players tended to have Skills they relied on more frequently than others.

She'd left a daisy chain of Soul Stone Shards, small, single-use devices, on her way through the Southlands.

They weren't very durable, as other Players or monsters could destroy them, but they lasted a week in real-time. The most frequent complaint about them was that Players couldn't respawn to them. They were available as teleport locations in the list, great for a quick run back to one of the major cities for a minute, but that was it.

Astra stared at her empty list.

What the heck?

She was some distance from the last one she'd dropped, and the others were older, leading up to the Player town at the edge of the Southlands, but that didn't explain why they were all gone.

"Ugh." Backing out of her teleport list, she moved to Inventory to get a Soul Stone Shard. That all of the ones she'd dropped in the last four game-time weeks were gone was only an inconvenience if she died. She wouldn't have a quick way back to her current location after respawning at the last major city she'd been in. The faster she got one activated, the better.

Astra activated the item and dropped it just as she heard shuffling in the bushes.

Looking up from her Menu, she met the eyes of a Razor Boar mid-charge. "[Dodge]" died on her lips as the two pairs of tusks ripped through her midsection. Pain like she had never felt before overwhelmed her senses. She collapsed to the ground. Her armor, which was as high-quality as she could make it, had protected her a bit from the attack, but the Boar continued to slash at her as she lay helpless on the ground, unable to think past the pain.

A tusk caught her in the throat, and a terrible coldness descended upon her.

Her consciousness hung suspended in darkness; before her were the options to Wait or Respawn. Choosing Respawn, her body exploded in sparks of light, teleporting back to the last Soul Stone she'd attuned to.

Astra wheezed out a moan of residual pain as her feet touched the pavement. Gripping herself, she shivered. Her pain setting must have gotten changed. Had they updated the game? Maybe that was why she'd passed out earlier.

She now stood in the Soul Stone Plaza of Aesir, a city built on the mountainous shore and sprawling onto an island within visual distance of the rocky beach. The architecture resembled ancient Greco-Roman, giving it an air of philosophical sophistication. It was her favorite city, and it looked gorgeous in the setting sun's light. However something was off.

Why was it so quiet?

Turning away from the Soul Stone, she found that the plaza, usually bustling with Players coming and going, was filled with market stalls and a crowd that was just trying to get their last bit of shopping done before it got too dark. While physically, Players and Non-Player Characters were identical, the system showed Player names to other Players in text hovering over their heads.

There were *no* Players in the crowd.

The stall owners and their customers stared at her, pale, jaws agape. A Human grandmother had dropped her basket of apples directly next to Astra. A Lycanth woman clutched her cub to her chest.

* * *

Something had changed today.

Since noon, he'd felt as if he'd been reconnected with something that had been missing for a very long time. He glanced up and right, checking the time. It was nearly seven in the evening. The sun would be setting soon.

"Divine Brother, is something wrong?"

He looked down at the young man who had been pestering him for the last fifteen minutes. Xander was on his way to the dining hall to get something to eat, but Prince Rufus el Aesir had popped in for a visit. Not to see the Holy Mouth, but Xander. Once again, he was disappointed by the people of Ashguard.

Prince Rufus stared up at him with deceptively clear blue eyes, his blond hair perfectly swept back from his forehead in the current noble style. While Xander had once been susceptible to this kind of innocent gaze, he'd grown weary of it two hundred years ago when he'd joined the Church of Leviathan. Just because the Cursed Ones were the most powerful beings on Ashguard didn't mean they needed to intervene in every petty squabble.

"No," Xander said. "I have given the matter some thought and humbly decline the opportunity."

"But we need you!" Rufus objected, hurrying to move in front of Xander, blocking his way. The boy was only sixteen, and so Xander couldn't bring himself to be too hard on him, but at the same time, pestering like this was rude.

"I am aware that you *think* you need me," Xander said, quick on the heels of the prince's whining. "However, you propose war with Vanaheim, and I have little interest in serving in another large-scale conflict."

"Your healing abilities are unmatched—"

Tired of the conversation, Xander walked away.

Being over five hundred years old had its advantages. He was *allowed* to walk away from conversations with royalty. Even though he wasn't the Holy Mouth, he'd held Prince Rufus's grandfather when he was in diapers at one point. Humans lived such short lives, but even Xander's Elven compatriots had withered and died of old age some time ago.

Xander was one of the Cursed Ones, having chosen to make a pact with an Immortal in his youth. Last he'd been told; there were only a few hundred left of them. He was undoubtedly one of the very few that decided to continue living a public life, despite the damage and disruption the others had caused when the Immortals had disappeared from the world.

"Please, our people will die in droves—"

"Then perhaps your father should rethink having a war."

"But—"

"[Stop]."

Rufus halted mid-stride, body unbalanced, but the magic prevented him from even blinking. Frozen in time and unable to protect himself, he helplessly watched as Xander looked him over with disgust. "Rufus el Aesir, know this: I *do not* answer to the monarchy of any kingdom, and I certainly do not answer to *incessant whining*. You would do well to learn how to state your case to me and accept the answer I give, regardless of whether you like it or not. Do not pester me again, boy." Turning away, Xander successfully walked away from the conversation, leaving Rufus to suffer through the remaining fifty-second duration of the spell by himself.

Xander inwardly sighed as the notification that his Stop Skill had leveled up appeared in his peripheral.

Rufus meant well. He had a good heart. He cared about his people's well-being, but he was still a child who didn't understand the consequences of the politics he was being used in. The Cursed One knew the king had put it into his son's head to ask Xander directly for help. He'd been a bit soft on the boy since he nearly died at birth.

Reaching the sanctuary, he stopped to stare up at the shrine to the Water Dragon Leviathan. Still, he couldn't pinpoint what was different about today.

Aside from Prince Rufus harassing him, there wasn't anything he could think of. War with Vanaheim had been on the table for ages. The flying city frequently levied high taxes on any caravans going through the forest below, regardless of whether the goods were headed to Vanaheim or Nifelheim beyond.

The recent increase in hostilities coincided with the Cursed One, Johnas, taking over the city ten years ago. That had been a surprising coup after many years of peace. Xander had thought that the fight over Vanaheim's throne had been done, but apparently, this guy thought not. While Cursed Ones could die, killing them wasn't easy. They'd had five hundred years to level up their Skills. Xander's Skills were all from the Healer Class, a Class rarely chosen by the Immortals. Johnas's was Warrior Class and then some.

Xander had met the man a long time ago, a Lycanth with multiple facial scars. He'd always been a crass, mouthy meathead, but his sudden play for power was just... different.

In any case, Xander wanted nothing to do with it.

He was a Healer. While he had the Raise Undead Skill, he detested using it; as such, he could only command a legion of fifty for a half hour. It had always been just enough time and resources to allow him to escape harm since his Immortal had disappeared. He didn't have the luxury of dying now that she was gone. There weren't many people with Healer Skills, as he could only make Scrolls that capped at level fifty. That was just enough to Resurrect someone with a few percentages of health. [Cure] at level fifty wasn't enough to keep someone alive during a fight and was best used after it was over.

He sighed.

Xander didn't miss those days of the endless war between Immortals, but he did miss her a little. She'd never spoken to him much and often seemed irritated that he needed anything. But she'd always Resurrected him as soon as possible and had kept him fed with the best food he'd ever had, even now. The clothes and armor she'd provided still outclassed anything he'd found to this day. She defended him from attack. She'd given him Skills that leveled infinitely. She'd had him carry her things and occasionally sell them on the Immortal Markets.

Life had been much simpler back then, despite the danger and exhaustion.

She would disappear for days, sometimes weeks, leaving him to fend for himself. Thankfully there were zones he could hide in that the Immortals couldn't enter or attack. But he always knew when she returned.

It felt like...

Xander gasped, his gaze flicking up and left. That space, which had been empty for so long, now held a ghostly green bar with Astra Diane's name beside it. Astra Diane's health dropped suddenly, then hit zero.

The acolyte who had been tending the Holy Waters nearby started, looking over at him.

Her health sparked and refilled with the red glow around her name to indicate she'd acquired a Death Penalty from respawning.

He knew instinctively that she was at the Soul Stone Plaza.

Clutching his heart, Xander rushed towards the sanctuary door, only to stop when the captain of the Royal Guard stepped in. The Giant man, resplendent in golden armor that glimmered in the waning daylight, rumbled, "Divine Brother, your presence is required by the king."

Damnation!

* * *

Astra breathed in, breathed out.

Usually, NPCs didn't give Players much notice; their AI didn't allow them to talk to Players. The crowd noise was another language. Even though Porters could understand commands, they only had a few phrases they could reply with. Astra's experience with Xander had been that he was helpful, such as picking up things she'd not asked him to or lending a hand in towns when fights with monsters took too long and other NPCs got hurt. She'd seen him give out meals to other NPCs. She frequently did this because they acted so startled and grateful.

She turned a full circle, looking around carefully, searching for the telltale green text of a Player's name and title.

A seagull honked overhead.

Pulling out her Menu, she opened Settings and Options. Where the heck were her HUD settings? Where were her Game settings? Where was Log Out?

Her tail thrashed in agitation, something it had never done in the past. Still, people were staring at her. She'd only ever had a vague awareness of having a tail while playing *Ashguard*, but now it really felt like it was part of her and had a mind of its own.

The wind whistled against the hairs in her ears. The sound of armored boots was unbearably loud. Five pairs, she could tell, moving in unison towards her. The crowd parted, allowing the troop of five city guards through, their spears leveled at Astra. The sun had fully set by now, leaving the plaza lit only by enchanted lanterns.

Clutching her useless Menu to her chest, Astra shrank back. She'd never seen the Aesir City Guard pull weapons on a Player before. Usually, they just walked in set paths around the city, patrolling, dealing with incidents between NPCs. Their low levels made them less than annoyances to a Player, which meant that bad apples frequently took advantage of the fact that they were practically gods among ants. Other Players had created guilds to police such activities since the NPCs didn't respawn.

Now that she was facing those spear tips, the thought of fleeing crossed her mind. But Astra knew it was useless. She had the Death Penalty, meaning she couldn't use Skills or Teleport. She was utterly helpless until it was removed or wore off in a few hours. Dying again with the Death Penalty still active would mean a hit to her stats, which were difficult to raise.

"I-is there s-something wrong...? Officers?" Astra tried saying. She targeted the guy in the front to see that he had a name, a male, tabby-colored Felis with mostly cat features.

The squad captain cleared his throat. "Did you just come from that Soul Stone?" he asked.

Astra looked up at the Soul Stone, then back at him. "Yes? I spawned here," she said. "I died in the Southlands." This was the weirdest conversation.

A collective gasp and rustle went through the crowd. They backed away further. A baby started crying. The Lycanth with her cub hurried off, retreating as if she thought she was in mortal danger.

"You—come with us," the squad captain said. He looked very uncomfortable saying that, but given everyone else's actions up until this point, he showed immense bravery in creeping toward her. "Put your hands up."

Astra closed her Menu, shoving it into her pocket, and put her hands up. Complying in the situation seemed like the best option.

The Felis guard grabbed one of her hands, bringing it down behind her, then the other, cuffing them together. "Please don't do anything," he said and nudged her forward. The crowd had started whispering. Her ears turned, catching snippets of conversation.

"Mommy, what's going on?" a child asked.

"What kind of person just appears out of a Soul

Stone?" an old man asked.

The crowd had come to life. Was this a massive update? The situation felt uncomfortably real. Astra was not enjoying this. "Where are we going? Why am I getting arrested?" Astra asked. "I don't understand why or what's going on?"

"I don't either," he admitted. "The Holy Mouth and king will figure it out," he said.

"Oh... okay," Astra said in a small voice. This had to be some kind of instance; a cut scene only she could see. That's what it was. An RP event she'd accidentally triggered! Her shoulders relaxed with relief that she'd finally figured it out, and she walked calmly with the guards. This must be a massive update where they finally put a story into the game—what a strange way to start a plotline, though. The NPCs were acting as if they'd never seen someone respawn from the Soul Stone before. If they were going with the angle that Players were new, four years into the game's release was a bit late...

The city looked different. It looked older. She didn't recall so much greenery on the buildings last time she was in Aesir.

Her guards looked more nervous the more relaxed she got. Maybe they had some dialog?

"I'm Astra," she said.

The Felis man looked back at her, his whiskers twitching. It looked like he wasn't going to answer. She couldn't see his ears because of his helmet, but his tail was puffy and flicking nervously. "Squad Captain Tensin," he said finally.

Astra nodded. "Nice to meet you." She focused on the

other four men: another mostly Human Felis, a Human man, and two Lycanth. Targeting each in turn, she found that they all had names too. Surely this wasn't a squad of Named NPCs? They had arrived at the foot of the stairs leading up to the nobility district.

Squad Captain Tensin pointed at one of his men. "Private Lloyd, alert the captain that we've taken her to the holding cells."

The human soldier saluted, running off at great speed.

Astra's tail flicked slightly. She would have preferred to go to the church where she could get the Death Penalty lifted, but this was a cut scene, and she couldn't exit out of it. She focused on the guard that stood next to the tower door at the base of the stairs, marking the wall between the nobility district and the merchant's area.

[Lieutenant Emmerson]

He had a name too?

Though time passed differently between the game world and the real world, she'd spent several hours in the Southland just gathering. It was probably time for her to get to bed. She had an opening shift at the QuickQ, and as much as she hated the place, it—barely—paid her bills.

Tensin stepped behind her and nudged her. Glancing up and around the dimly lit guardroom, she found stone walls, a worn-down wooden floor, and a table and chairs set to the side as a break area for guards. Stairs led downward across the room, where Tensin took her.

Carefully moving down the wooden stairs, Astra folded her ears back again when a spiderweb hit her across the eyes. Shaking her head, she wrinkled her nose, trying to get the sticky feeling off, and finally resorted to rubbing her face with her shoulder as best she could. At the bottom of the stairs, they turned right. Tensin pushed her forward.

Astra caught her balance a few steps in, tripping on the worn cobblestones. She turned around just as he locked the metal bars closed.

"Will you uncuff me?" she asked.

Tensin's tail flicked in agitation. "No."

"I can't do anything," Astra pointed out.

He walked away.

Ears folded down again, Astra sighed. How long was this going to take? Her eyes roamed the tiny cell. A bench across the back wall provided a seat but little else in the way of accommodations.

She sat down.

* * *

Xander stood before the king in his study. He knew he'd passed Astra Diane on his way to the palace. She'd been taken to the holding cells at the edge of the markets, which confused him. Why had she been arrested?

"I'll cut straight to business," King James said. "We need your help."

"I told your son no," Xander interrupted. "But I suspect you didn't give him time to report my answer."

King James sighed. "I didn't send him."

"Of course you didn't," Xander said flatly, clasping his hands behind him. "Have you considered that perhaps war with Vanaheim is not a good idea?"

"I'm getting pressured by the Merchants' Guild. These tariffs are going too far."

"Then find some political way to negotiate with Johnas," Xander suggested.

"I've tried!" James said, slamming his fist on the table as he stood. "He's only allowed one emissary to return with his head still attached. He's demanding that Aesir become a vassal state."

Xander shook his head. "War is not going to fix the problem."

"Then what would you have me do? Kill Johnas? How? We don't compare to a Cursed One's power, and you, the only one openly in Aesir, are refusing to get involved."

Xander remained unmoved. He couldn't care less. His mind was on Astra Diane. Her Death Penalty would wear off soon. What kind of trouble would she cause? He'd never heard of an Immortal being locked in a cell before. Would she be offended? He didn't think she would put up with it for long, even if she'd never intentionally destroyed things the way other Immortals had.

James stared at Xander helplessly.

"I've been informed that a woman appeared at the Soul Stone Plaza," James said.

"An Immortal," Xander said.

"You knew?"

"I was aware the moment she revived there," Xander said.

James rubbed his forehead, pulling the crown off his forehead to set it on his desk. It had left a ring indention, which combined with his balding was not a flattering look.

"I'd suggest not keeping her locked up for much longer. Immortals are frequently unpredictable and can be violent. Their power exceeds Cursed Ones because killing them is only an inconvenience," Xander said.

"Would she be willing to help—?"

"I can't answer for her," Xander said, already deciding that he would try to keep Astra Diane away from the politics. "But involving her in any battles within city limits would result in many casualties."

She was Healer Class, but her Raise Undead was an army in and of itself last he remembered. She won fights with monsters by whittling them down and continuously Curing herself. Unfortunately, that led to a lot of collateral damage. She did at least try to lure monsters out of populated areas whenever she fought them, but still... She just wasn't very good at it, and Xander usually took on the task of making sure any innocent people were out of the way and healed while she played bait. The idea of her fighting Johnas was... not pleasant. He'd destroy the entire city of Vanaheim before he died.

Xander glanced up and left as a flash of light let him know that her Death Penalty had just worn off. He needed out of this damn office.

"Your time is running out to decide the Immortal's fate," Xander said. "She may decide to break herself out at any moment."

James pushed his hands across his balding head. "Fine. Go deal with her."

Xander bowed out of politeness and turned, leaving the room.

* * *

Bored.

Boring.

Incredibly boring.

Astra sighed and shifted on the bench. She'd given up sitting and laid down. Now instead of her butt hurting, her shoulder and hip were in pain. This was the worst story!

It had been long enough that her Death Penalty had worn off on its own, which meant that she'd sat in this hole for hours in real life. It was well past her bedtime. She couldn't access her Menu because her hands were tied behind her, so she couldn't Log Out, and she couldn't even fix her armor, which had been torn to shreds by the Razor Boar. Her health had returned with her respawn, but blood still soaked the leather armor and shredded clothes beneath. She shivered in the chill cell. This was a new experience too. She'd never been cold in the game before. It felt like this was her real body, down to the grumbling of her stomach and hunger pains.

Flicking her tail against her leg, she growled in the darkness. This was bull.

She sat up and turned to the door. Maybe she was supposed to interact with it? Perhaps she'd misunderstood the story cues? She examined the door, but the bars did not indicate what she should do with it. No helpful text popped up that said [Pick Lock] or something similar.

Astra kicked it, feeling the jolt of kicking sturdy metal through her boot.

The door rattled, the clanging of metal-on-metal echoing in the holding cells and up the stairs.

"I need to go to bed," she whined. She figured she was so tired in real-time that she'd started to feel tired in-game. It was making her cranky.

She kicked the door again.

"Oi! Quiet down there!" someone shouted from above.

Folding her ears down, Astra tapped her foot on the floor. She'd not wanted to resort to destroying things, but this was just too much. If there was one thing she'd learned over the last four years of playing, some structures were destructible. Maybe this door was one of them?

Turning around, she put her hands against the lock. "[Ice Bullet]." This was a relatively new Skill for her. It wouldn't damage much, but maybe she could chip away at its durability. She'd accidentally come across the Skill Master before the plague had started to spread, a lucky break, considering how difficult it was to find Skill Masters for anything, let alone standard Skills for other Classes.

Peeking back to check the lock, she found the frost quickly melting away. Astra kicked the door again. It didn't budge. Admittedly, she could have used Raise Undead, but that would've been far messier. She'd save that Skill for when she needed it.

"[Haste]," she cast. "[Ice Bullet], [Ice Bullet], [Ice Bullet], [Fire Bullet]." Her ice bullets hit the lock and bounced off. The fire bullet fizzled on contact.

"Oi! What're you doing down there?" the guard above shouted. She heard his feet crossing the wooden floor above.

"[Fire Bullet], [Fire Bullet], [Fire Bullet]." Her Haste wore off. Astra mule-kicked the door as hard as she could.

It banged but did not budge.

The guard stomped down the stairs, crouching to look at her from the stairs. He was a large Lycanth with a humanoid face and tawny fur growing from his head and down his shoulders. "You ain't gonna get out with that, girlie," he said. "Lock's been warded against Elemental Mastery."

With that, her escape attempt was effectively thwarted. She didn't have any levels in Debuff. "Why am I arrested anyway?" she asked.

"Well, the higher-ups gotta have some reason," the guard said, scratching the side of his head. "An' considerin' you are trying to escape, they're probably right to lock you up."

Astra folded her ears down. "I've done nothing wrong! At least uncuff me? I obviously can't get out."

"Nope," the Lycanth said. He stood, turned, and headed back up the stairs.

"Aarrhhh!" Astra kicked the door again. "This is bull!"

She was about to throw herself down on the bench again when a clatter above resounded through the floor. Footsteps thumped across to the stairs, and the bottom hem of deep blue and gold robes came into view.

The Elven man that descended the stairs was a vision of icy beauty, his long, silver hair shining like stars against his pale skin. Eyes the color of icebergs shot straight through her.

"Xander!" she greeted. How nice to see him! She'd wondered where he'd been. Usually, he would show up within minutes of her appearing back in town. It must have been part of the story. He'd changed his clothes to a Church of Leviathan Brother's robe. Once held back in a tail, his hair hung in sheets of silver down his back and across one shoulder as he leaned on the railing.

Her Porter's cold expression didn't change in the slightest. Not that she'd expected it to. He turned around and went back up the stairs, swishing his robes out of the way with long, graceful fingers.

"Hey—" Astra objected and pressed herself against the bars, trying to peer after him. "Hey! Don't ignore me!" She slid her face down the gritty bars with a defeated groan. "This event sucks!"

* * *

Shaking head to toe, Xander strode out of the guard room and into the street. The enchanted lamps around the square couldn't entirely dispel the shadows that clung heavily as night set in.

Her onyx face hadn't changed a bit since the last time he'd seen her, speckled with white freckles across her nose, her bright green eyes contrasting with her stark white hair. She was short for a Felis and well-endowed, a beautiful Immortal, like all of them had been.

Unfortunately, Xander couldn't help but be terrified. If *she* was back, did that mean they were *all* back? Was the Eternal War going to start again? Clenching his fingers into fists to hide their shaking, he stood in the street. The guard who had brought her in stood awkwardly nearby. The Royal Guard captain also waited.

"So?" the gruff Giant prodded. "What's the verdict?"

He would have to do *something* about her. He couldn't leave her down there. But letting her roam free was out of the question. Xander turned to look at the Felis guard. "She appeared at the Soul Stone?" he asked.

24

"Yes, according to witnesses. She appeared in a flash of light. She told me she died in the Southlands," the Felis guard said, tail twitching in agitation.

Witnesses. Which meant that news could get around to other Cursed Ones. There would be no hiding this.

Xander nodded and forced himself to take a steadying breath. Had she been in the Southlands the whole time? No. He'd felt her die. The sudden severing of their Pact had brought him to his knees. It was a feeling of sudden emptiness that tugged at him constantly. He'd spent the first several hundred years drinking to block out that ache, then replaced drink with endless work so he couldn't think about it. How had he not noticed it was gone for most of the day?

He finally said, "Release her into my custody. I will ensure that she causes no trouble." Xander knew that his usual icy demeanor covered most of his thoughts and emotions, but he also knew that this had rattled him so much that he was not doing an excellent job hiding how terrified he was. Even the brutish idiot Royal Guard captain had begun to pick up on it.

The Felis had scented his fear the moment Xander had walked past him. The guard hesitated, looking from Xander to the Royal Guard captain, obviously unsure of what to do.

"Maybe we should keep her—"

"I know this one," Xander interrupted. "She is generally tame, but I know her power. She will remain in that cell only as long as she desires to." Striding across the cobblestones, he came to stand beneath the Royal Guard captain, looking up at him sternly. "Immortals are not kind. They are not benevolent. They are destructive and endlessly powerful. Death is only a minor inconvenience to them. Do not mistake this one's docility as weakness." He saw the Felis guard move from his peripheral but didn't break eye contact with the Giant before him.

"Then that's more reason to keep her locked up!" the Royal Guard shouted.

"Immortals do not care about us," Xander insisted. "If she wants out, she will get out. Leaving her in there will only anger her, and then all of us will suffer."

"I don't have the authority—" the Royal Guard started.

"Divine Brother," the Felis City Guard said, drawing Xander's attention.

He stood at the door with the Immortal before him. Her hands were still locked behind her back, her tail flicking, ears laid back, though her face was unreadable. The animation of her tail and ears was unusual. Xander had only ever seen her use her face to emote feelings. Had something happened?

She looked like she'd had a rough death. The entire front of her armor was ripped out. Her usual gorget had fallen off entirely. The armor hung like a coat on her, barely preserving her modesty. She had goosebumps on her onyx skin, belying that she was cold. The weirdest part was that she seemed to be aware of what they were saying as if she could actually understand them, a marked difference from the last time he'd had the displeasure of interacting with an Immortal outside of receiving simple commands.

"Release her bindings," Xander ordered.

The Felis hesitated, but only for a second.

Once her hands were free, the Immortal pulled them forward to rub her wrists and roll her shoulders. She adjusted the hang of her torn and bloody armor to cover herself better. "About time," she muttered. "I need to go." Reaching for her pocket, she pulled out a Scroll. Opening it, she scanned it with her eyes. "Why can't I log out?" she asked. "This is nuts." She looked up as Xander approached. "Did you finish selling—?"

"Be still," he told her firmly, mustering everything he had to dare to command an Immortal.

She pursed her lips, ears flicking sideways in shock.

He had her full attention. It was an unusual feeling. He'd spent nearly eight years with her. Sometimes she talked at him or herself, but her words had always been noises that didn't resemble words. He'd tried talking to her a few times, but she either didn't hear him or his words made no sense to her either. The only time clear communication had come through was when she gave him a command, such as "stand here" or "go there." Now, she was speaking sounds that were clearly words, even if he had no idea what she meant by them.

"W-what?" she asked, finally deciding that she wanted to be annoyed. "Be still? What's that supposed to mean? Are you telling me to shut up?"

Xander did something he never thought he would ever do. He took the Scroll from her hands. "Astra Diane," he said firmly. "Be silent and follow me. You are in my custody, but I will not tolerate any destructive behavior from you. Is that clear?"

She grasped her empty hands in shock several times, seemingly unable to comprehend what had just happened.

"I just need to log out," she said.

"No," Xander answered. "You will not log out for the time being." He put her Scroll into his pocket. Dangerous as it was, he turned his back on her and started walking. "Come." He didn't know what "log out" meant, but if it was when she temporarily didn't exist in the world, then he couldn't allow that until he got some answers. Perhaps now that they could clearly understand each other he could interrogate her. The idea was absurd. Ordinary people didn't just talk to Immortals.

After several steps, he heard the pitter of her tiny feet as she jogged to catch up to him. "You're being rude," she said, clutching the remains of her armor closed over her breasts. "Give my Menu back. How did you take it? You're not allowed to do that." She sounded more confused than anything. "What do you mean I can't Log Out? You can't keep me here."

She pattered up next to him, grasping his sleeve with a slight tug. "Please. I've got obligations in the morning. I need to Log Out."

"Obligations?" Xander asked, stopping in his tracks. "An Immortal with *obligations*?"

Her ears flattened once more. "Xander. Give me my Menu," she ordered. "Don't make me kill you and take it off your corpse."

"All those years I followed you," he said, heart in his throat. "I never once thought you capable of such cruelty. You are exactly like the others." He didn't know how serious her threat was, but it would be easier to handle her if her Skills were locked.

Astra Diane stared up at him in confusion, only to

grunt as his knife stabbed through her ribs. It was a gamble as to whether the item could take her down. He'd seen her defend herself from other Immortals before.

To his surprise, she died.

Her corpse hit the ground, rested there for a moment, then exploded in light.

Xander changed his path, heading towards the Soul Stone. She would respawn there, he knew. He also knew that he could find her wherever she went. Running was not an option.

* * *

She couldn't believe what had just happened.

Her Porter had knifed her!

Astra sat on the ground at the Soul Stone, seething. The crowd from earlier had all dispersed. Only empty stalls remained as a witness to her respawn. Thankfully, her Death Penalty from before had worn off, but now she had a new one, and if she died again while it was active, her stats would take the hit.

"He killed me!" Porters weren't supposed to be able to do that! Porters just followed you around and carried your stuff. Sure, sometimes Xander had done things outside of the commands she'd actively given, but that was just his AI trying to be helpful. She'd had him focused on casting [Cure] and [Resurrect] if she died. She'd never given him any Melee Skills since the only Melee Skill she had was a Player Scroll with Dual Wield. Astra had not leveled that up enough to make a Skill Scroll of her own to give him. If she'd had her Menu she would have been able to check

29

her Skill levels and his, but since he'd taken it, she was completely blind.

Furthermore, he killed her with a simple knife, which meant that his STR was probably higher than hers. She pulled her ruined armor tighter around her chest. If her armor had been intact, she was sure he wouldn't have been able to do that.

She heard footsteps approaching but didn't bother looking. Of course, he knew where she was. Where else would she have been?

"Get up," Xander ordered.

Turning to scowl up at him, Astra couldn't think of anything to say. He'd killed her, and while it wasn't permanent, it was indeed painful. If she could just find the Menu options to fix that... but she didn't have her Menu!

He pulled the knife out again. "I know you don't like dying multiple times in a row. Get up."

Astra got up. She tried to control her expression, but her ears were pinned back, and her tail lashed. She had no choice. Her Skills and Teleportation were locked. Even if her Teleportation wasn't locked, he *had her Menu*!

She couldn't even pull out one of her weapons to defend herself physically; that was only available through her Menu. She'd died in the Southlands with pruning shears equipped. She couldn't switch weapons.

"Would you be reasonable?" Astra asked. "I need to Log Out." The whole idea of this was absurd. She was arguing with her Porter!

"I implore you to be reasonable," Xander said. "Allowing you to leave now is not an option. I intended to have this discussion somewhere more private, but your threat of slaughtering me forced my hand."

"Forced your hand?" Astra shouted, throwing her arms up. "You knifed me!" She turned to walk away, only to be yanked back by her arm, the knife pressed against her throat. She stared into the icy gaze of her NPC.

"And I will do so again," Xander said. "As many times as it takes. You are too dangerous to allow to walk free."

"D-dangerous?" she sputtered. None of this made sense.

"Astra Diane, how many times have you died in this Plaza to other Immortals? Immortals, who were not even targeting you but merely destroying the city?" Xander demanded. At least the knife moved away from her throat, but his grip on her arm was tight.

She glanced around. Admittedly, she'd died many times, and so had Xander. She'd had to drag his corpse out of the city to get away from the stupidity and wait for her Death Penalty to wear off before she could Resurrect him. But wait... That had been fights between Players. Maybe from an NPC's point of view, Players were immortal, she supposed. "Where are the others?" she asked. "I don't see anyone else here."

"They have been absent for five hundred years," Xander said. "However, your reappearance implies that others might follow."

Astra stared at him, her tail stilling its furious lashing. "Five... hundred? But... I wasn't gone... did they update, and I didn't know?" she wondered.

"Come," Xander said, releasing her arm finally and stepping back. "We will speak further somewhere more private." He started walking without looking back to see if she was following.

Astra sighed, feeling incredibly weird about following her Porter, but jogged to catch up and walked a step behind and beside. He was leading her to the church. "Why not the inn?" she asked.

"And expose more innocents to danger should you decide to Raise Undead?" Xander asked.

"I wouldn't do that," Astra said. "And I wouldn't have actually killed you."

"Considering that this is the first time we've spoken to each other, I can't say I know you well enough to believe that." The look he gave her from the corner of his eye was chilly. She was not going to get an apology for the knifing.

Astra folded her arms, muttering curses at him under her breath as she followed him up the white staircase.

As they approached the doors to the sanctuary, an acolyte hurried up, blue robes fluttering. "Divine Brother," the young Elven girl said. "The Holy Mouth wishes to speak to you."

Xander looked from the acolyte to Astra. Coming to a decision, he said, "Heather, take this woman to my apartment. Give her food and clothes." He looked at Astra. "You are to stay there until I return. I'm sure you're aware that I can find you wherever you go in this world."

Ears folding down, Astra felt like she'd barely had them up at all today. "Fine," she growled. She did want some time to herself to think about how to deal with this unusually willful NPC. Turning, she looked at the acolyte and gestured for her to go on.

Heather bowed to Xander, then Astra, her confusion evident. Taking the lead, she headed into the church while

Xander peeled off in a different direction.

"Why do you call him 'Divine Brother'?" Astra asked as they turned right into a long hallway. This was a section she'd never been in before. Previous forays into the church to get her Death Penalty removed had always ended at the altar. Side halls like this one had been roped off.

"Because he is one of the church," the girl said. "He has had ample opportunity to become the Holy Mouth but has declined the honor, remaining a Brother within our order. His powers are far beyond ours, so out of respect, we've given him a new title. You are lucky to have a personal audience with him. He does not often speak to others." She folded her hands in her wide sleeves, flushing slightly.

Sensing that she could get more information out of this NPC, Astra moved closer. "Doesn't talk to others?" she asked. "Why?"

"He is a lonely soul," Heather said. "As one of the Cursed Ones, he is blessed with eternal youth and Skills that know no bounds, but he must watch Time take all except him in return."

Heather stopped at the door and gestured. "We have arrived." Opening the door, she allowed Astra to enter. "I shall bring meal and clothes shortly."

Entering, Astra looked around the spacious sitting room. It was nice but a bit sterile. One wall consisted of shelves stuffed with books and other knickknacks. A boat in a bottle caught her eye, and she approached, touching it with a finger to use Examine.

[Boat in a Bottle Level 200, Crafter Astra Diane]

She turned to look around the room again, approaching

the couch. Touching it, she used Examine.

[White Rosewood Settee Level 100, Crafter Astra Diane]

She frowned. "I told him to sell this."

A sigh escaped her. Without her Menu, she couldn't even see how much longer she had to wait for the Death Penalty to wear off. Her tail lashed.

"That jerk knifed me."

* * *

Xander didn't have to bow to the Holy Mouth, but he did so out of courtesy. "You wished to speak to me," he said, closing the door to her office.

The Holy Mouth, a wizened Dracoid, nervously twiddled a pen between her claws where she sat behind her desk. "You brought the Immortal here," she said.

"Yes. I deemed it the safest way to keep an eye on her," Xander said.

Standing, the Holy Mouth put the pen down. "I was told you slaughtered her in the street."

"I did," Xander admitted. He still couldn't believe he'd done that.

"And yet here she is, in our church, undamaged."

"Immortals have some inconvenience when they are killed," Xander explained. "For a time, their Skills are locked. They must either be blessed by the Holy Waters or simply wait for the effect to wear off."

"So, the Immortal is disarmed at the moment," the Holy Mouth said.

"For the moment," Xander agreed. "I believe reasoning

with her is possible."

"Is she likely to side with us in the coming war?"

Irritated that the conversation had taken this turn, Xander bit his tongue to prevent himself from saying anything he might regret later. After a moment, he took a breath and said, "Her decisions are her own to make. However, I would caution against asking an Immortal to take sides. They are unpredictable and dangerous."

"Yet you brought one here."

"Where else would I take her?" Xander snapped. "I've disarmed her to the best of my abilities. She is cooperative for now."

"Xander, you know that we are facing a Cursed One. We will lose many good people to his Skills without your help."

"So, you think turning to an Immortal will solve the problem? I lived in the time of the Immortals, Grestra. Yes, they called themselves 'Adventurers' and took on requests at the guild, but how they performed their tasks were often unexpected. I've seen many instances where a mere potion was requested but Astra Diane delivered an Elixir. Removal of rats in the sewers often ended with the entire system being blasted sterile with fire!" Frustrated that he could not make these people understand the dangers Immortals represented, Xander fell silent.

"You are against even asking her," Grestra said.

"Do as you please," he muttered. "I will be removing myself from the church tomorrow."

"Xander!" she gasped and stepped around her desk, reaching out for him. "Please, do not make hasty decisions!"

"You are all fools," he said coldly. "Johnas has merely raised taxes, and you would throw lives away in protest of them. A war between the Cities has not happened in ages, and you would drag me into one regardless of my protests."

"With the Immortal on our side, we need not involve you."

"You would involve me," Xander said firmly. "Astra Diane was the Immortal I served. Where she goes, I am bound to follow." He stared the Dracoid woman down.

Admittedly, he could stay in Aesir, but that would hardly keep him from being involved in the conflict if the fighting came here. His best bet, he realized, would be to allow her to Log Out with the promise to never return. However, if she was here, the problem remained, then other Immortals were likely in the world again.

Astra Diane had only ever acted to defend herself when attacked, but he had seen her summon creatures in city limits before. She wasn't incapable of causing destruction.

This time, he did not bow. Xander let himself out of the Holy Mouth's office and stalked across the compound.

Why could no one see the bigger picture in all this? Johnas was a mere pebble in the shoe compared to an Immortal, and now Xander had the arduous task of deciding whether trying to get rid of Astra Diane was the right thing to do. She would be the only thing capable of taking on another Immortal. However, their battle would be endless, as they could not die permanently. Not to mention that her Class was Healer, which did not lend itself to combat. Pausing in the hall outside his apartment door, Xander pulled out the Scroll he'd taken from her. It was something he'd seen her consult often but never had the opportunity to look at himself.

Opening it, Xander hoped he was prepared for whatever happened.

* * *

Astra squinted, then swatted her ear as the soft sounds of the room suddenly became unbearably loud for a moment. True to her word, the acolyte had brought a simple meal and clothes. She had intended to ignore the meal, but her stomach had rumbled upon smelling it. Was this a new feature to the game?

The food itself was plain, but it filled her, and afterward, Astra wandered the apartment once over, finding a well-appointed bathroom, bedroom, and office, all with views of a lush garden that looked out over the ocean.

After, she'd returned to the sitting room and sprawled on the couch, fingers laced on her belly as she stared at the ceiling.

The door opened. Twisting, Astra looked back to see Xander entering, looking... impassive and cold. "Did you have fun?" she asked sarcastically.

Xander came to stand next to her head and stared down at her. "I wish to know more about your obligations," he said and stepped back to sit in the chair opposite.

She stared at him, watching as his hands gripped the arms of his chair, the only sign that something was going on in his head. He'd always had these little habits he did, but now that she knew he wasn't just an AI, it was disconcerting. When she'd picked him, she'd only done so because he was pretty to look at since she knew she'd be hauling his butt around all creation for a very long time. Then again, maybe he'd always been like this, and she hadn't noticed? However, His Iceness was annoying.

"Give me my Menu," she said, holding her hand towards him.

"I will not," Xander said. He pulled something else out of his pocket and placed it into her waiting hand—a vial of Holy Water.

Astra brought it closer but kept her eyes on him. The distrust was palpable. Sitting up, she folded her legs in a cross and set the bottle on the coffee table between them. "You're acting very weird," she said.

"Everything you do is strange," Xander said. "But I believe I begin to understand."

"Really?" Astra asked coyly, tipping her head. "How about you run it by me?"

Silence fell between them, and she watched Xander struggle to find the questions he wanted to ask first. "When you Log Out, you go somewhere else. Where is that?"

She shrugged. "The real world. My boring life." She kept a close eye on him, though. What would happen if she told him he was an NPC in a game?

"This existence," he gestured at her, "Is not your natural state."

"Nope. It's an avatar I control when I come here."

"Log Out allows you to close your connection to this avatar," Xander said.

He smelled stressed, she realized, afraid... Terrified.

"Our world is a playground for your kind," Xander

concluded.

Folding her ears down, Astra was not sure she liked how this conversation was going. "Well... yeah?"

"Then the countless lives that have been taken. The battles between Immortals... there was no point except wanton destruction."

"Probably," Astra admitted. "I just wanted to see the story," she defended. "Those other Players were just jerks."

"The... story..." Xander choked. He stood abruptly and left the room. She watched the office door close and frowned in thought.

She sat in silence, staring at the door.

Xander was acting like he was alive... aware. This was a massive update to the game if they'd suddenly given all the NPCs voices and names like this. Surely, they hadn't named every last person in Ashguard? The weirder option was that Ashguard was a world of its own that Earth had accidentally interacted with through VR. That was downright laughable. An update didn't explain why she couldn't log out, though.

Astra looked at the Holy Water on the coffee table. Most of the decor in this apartment was products of her Crafting. Surely, she wasn't so great a Player that the game admin had decided to make her Porter into a central figure in the plot. Players like Lancelot Valor or Patricia Penelope would've been better candidates. They'd impacted the world of Ashguard, either policing Player behavior where the game's controls couldn't—like Lancelot—or by protecting the NPCs from Player abuses the way Patricia had. And there were other, higher-level

Healers out there, she was sure. She'd just never really heard of many since Healer Class wasn't picked often due to lack of DPS capabilities.

Being trapped in a video game was something that only happened in stories.

However, the possibility that she *was* stuck worried her some. If she was stuck, what had happened to her body? Would she be forcibly disconnected when someone took the visor off her face? Would anyone even go looking for her before she started to rot? It wasn't like she had friends who checked up on her. The QuickQ might call her if she didn't show up for a shift, but that was probably the extent to which they'd look for her.

She didn't like the idea of just starving to death while her mind was stuck in a VR world because while death in Ashguard wasn't permanent for her, death on Earth certainly was. She needed to log out.

To do so, she would need Xander's cooperation.

Picking up the vial of Holy Water, she took it with her as she followed him to the office. Xander stood with his back to the door, propped by his palms on his desk, head hung. "Then what was I?" he asked. "You chose to keep me around, yet you ignored my presence." His fingers curled on the desk, dragging his nails across the wood.

Astra approached cautiously, setting the bottle down where he could see that she'd not used it. "You were my Porter," she said honestly. "Xan... something strange has happened. I'm... more connected than I've ever felt while playing. Something has changed, and maybe not for the better. The way I'm connected to this world leaves my real body just... laying there. If I don't go back to it, there's a possibility I'll die for real here. And I understand that Players weren't the greatest influence on this world, if... if, in fact, this place is actually a real place and not a game like we all thought."

Xander took a deep breath, held it, then let it out. "Astra Diane, you are a monster," he told her. "Your ilk are all a blight upon this world. We have had relative peace for five hundred years, but if you are here, would that not mean that there are more?" He pushed off the desk and turned to look down at her. "For five hundred years, I have endeavored to keep the peace in this city, stabilize the government, give hope to the people that the days of senseless slaughter were over... and I am tired. But for you to brazenly admit that all this has been a game... I am unsure I can go on."

Astra rubbed her eye with her hand, heaving a sigh. "Okay. Yeah. It's a lot to take in," she admitted. "But was I really that bad?"

"Anytime you fought monsters, you never seemed to give much thought to the collateral damage you caused. I appreciate that you didn't command me to lure the monster away, but you were very slow about defeating them, and the casualties were always more than I could handle by myself. You Resurrected people after the fact but allowing them to die in the first place was cruel."

Cringing, Astra looked away. "Okay, that's... pretty bad." She didn't even remember that particular quest, which made it all the worse.

Letting her breath out, she said, "I can't change the past, but I can change how I act in the future. That's all I can promise."

"If you are able to Log Out, will you leave for good?" Xander asked.

"If there are other Players, me logging out and staying out isn't going to change anything," Astra pointed out, then looked around. "I'd miss getting to see you. And Aesir is beautiful when it's not on fire... and I was exploring the Southlands..." She curled her fingers into her palms. "I'm still not sure I even believe that this is more than a game."

Shifting uncomfortably, Astra found the strength to meet his icy gaze. "Let me check my Menu?"

"Log Out would be an option in it, correct?" Xander asked. "It is not there."

Astra felt cold. He had looked at her Menu. It wasn't like she had any personal information there, but it felt weird knowing that someone else had looked through something only she had ever been able to touch. All her Quest Logs, her stats, the horrible mess in her Inventory... "You messed with the audio," she said, realizing. "At least that works still. Did you see Pain Tolerance options?"

"Yes," Xander said.

"That's good."

"I could not change the percentage," he said.

"That's not good."

"You have a new Skill," Xander said.

"Elemental Mastery," Astra agreed. "Just got it. I'll share once I get it leveled up enough. Did you want the other ones?"

"Why are they locked at one hundred?"

"They're Skills I bought from other Players," Astra said. "If I made a Scroll for those Skills and gave them to you, you'd only be able to level them to one hundred as

well. Skills I get from the guild or a Skill Master have no cap."

Xander nodded slightly. He seemed to have calmed down.

But the problem still hung between them: Was it or was it not a game?

* * *

She left the room, went back to the settee, and dropped onto it. After a moment, she slid sideways and sighed. She had left the Holy Water on his desk. Her Death Penalty would wear off in a few more hours anyway, but Xander appreciated the gesture. She had come to speak with him completely disarmed, despite how uncomfortable the conversation had been for them both.

Xander closed the door. He needed to think.

Her admissions explained a lot about how the Immortals had acted. They didn't see the world of Ashguard as a real place. They entered and exited it at their convenience and obviously did not believe that the people living there, even their closest companions, were real people.

Moving to his chair, Xander sat and leaned his elbows on the desk, head bowed.

Although that didn't explain some of her behavior towards him during those seven-plus years he'd followed her. He knew she didn't need sleep, but sometimes he would wake up to find her curled against him. Back then... he'd been convinced that she felt miserably alone, and even though they couldn't communicate verbally, the warmth of an embrace transcended any language barrier.

He'd been glad to hold her then, especially in the small cold hours of the night.

He'd been more than glad if he was being honest with himself. A creature that couldn't die had turned to him when she felt alone and vulnerable. Xander had never felt more powerful than in those moments, and he'd spent years searching for that euphoria after she'd died. Now that she was back... did he really want her to go? Now that the constant ache of her death had been soothed, he finally felt like he could think clearly.

What difference would it make if she did leave and never came back? Others—the less reasonable Immortals—would likely take the information that this world was alive and increase their destruction. The only way to safeguard the world would be to get rid of the Immortals entirely and prevent them from ever returning. That was certainly a tall order, considering they couldn't be killed permanently.

Reaching over, he pulled the bottle of Holy Water closer, rolling it along its edge.

The things the Immortals could achieve, though... They could craft high-quality items in seconds that exceeded the efforts of even the most renowned master craftsman. Astra Diane's Crafting Skills alone would destroy the market. Her other Skills were high, but she wasn't that good compared to his. In fact, he'd surpassed her levels some time ago in the Skills she'd shared with him. The only thing she was still better at than him was Raise Undead.

Hells, the amount of Fen she had stashed would crash the economy! He had handled selling items for her in the past, and honestly, he'd been astonished at the prices she'd set. The only saving grace was that the things he sold went to other Immortals who could afford to drop two hundred thousand Fen on a couch.

More proof that Immortals don't care about the actual value of anything.

He would give the Menu back to her. There was little point in keeping it, Xander decided. He needed her to work with him to find a way to save Ashguard from the Immortals. It was bad enough the Cursed Ones, those who had once walked beside the Immortals as glorified pack mules, were capable of so much destruction. If he could rid the world of his kind as well, Xander had to admit he would gladly do so.

Standing, he pocketed the Holy Water and headed back into the sitting room only to stop when he found Astra Diane asleep on the couch.

He had dragged himself after her for years despite how utterly exhausted he was, all because an Immortal's energy knew no bounds. She could jog for days without rest, and he wasn't sure what prompted her to stop and tell him to make camp, but he was grateful for it. His only consolation was that she would disappear and leave him for weeks at a time before reappearing and continuing the slog. Admittedly, the best part about traveling with her was that she made the best food. He absolutely missed her cooking.

Astra Diane snorted and kicked her foot.

She did not sleep gracefully, that was for certain.

* * *

She started awake at the sound of a door and glanced at the time on the upper right of her vision. It was six in the morning.

Astra pried her eyes open and wiped her face with her hand. She felt... greasy... she smelled like body odor... and she realized she needed to pee. That was a first, for sure. She'd never needed to sleep, eat, or rest while playing before. After her brief self-inspection, she looked up to find Xander standing over her, looking down his perfect, straight nose at her.

This felt far too real to be just a game anymore.

When she'd first gotten him, she often forgot that Xander was there, following silently behind her until the system reminded her. That had been surprising the first time. For a while after, she'd found it mildly annoying since it slowed her down. But as work got worse for the holiday season, she'd been glad for that downtime. She'd combed his hair and braided it because it always felt so silky in her hands, and it was calming. She'd even gone so far as to climb into his bedroll with him just because she needed a hug after a long day of getting abused by awful customers at the QuickQ. He would always roll over in his sleep and hold her. She'd watched him sleep countless times.

Given his expression now, it seemed the tables were turned. He had gotten to watch her sleep. She burst out laughing. She laughed until she snorted and wiped tears from her eyes.

"Do Immortals sleep in the other realm?" he asked.

"Yeah," Astra said. "It was my favorite thing to do. Other than hanging out in Ashguard."

He grunted. Pulling something from his pocket, he held a Scroll out to her.

Recognizing her Menu, Astra took it and stuck it into her pocket, choosing to believe that he had looked for her Log Out option and not found one.

"There are fresh clothes for you and a bath waiting. Please make use of them," Xander said.

"All right, all right," Astra muttered and stood, giving a good long stretch that had her joints cracking in chorus. Finishing with a yawn, Astra took herself to the bathroom she'd found earlier to take care of personal hygiene. According to her time sense, it had to have been around twelve hours since she'd put on the headset and laid down to play. Ashguard's time was an hour for every thirty minutes in real-time. She would need to get up soon if she was going to make it to her shift at the QuickQ.

She pulled out her Menu in the bath to calmly look it over.

Inventory, Character, Stats, Porter...

Curious, she opened the Porter tab. "Cheese and crust, look at those levels!" she gasped. He outclassed her in everything except Raise Undead and the Crafting Skills. If they battled a monster anytime soon, *she* would be the liability.

Continuing to the System Settings tab, she swiped through. As Xander had said, the pain tolerance was greyed out. There was only one slider for audio instead of three. No more background music for her.

She touched the slider, adjusting it back to where she was comfortable. There were no other options. That was it. Log Out did not exist. Not even greyed out. There wasn't even a space for it.

She did have the option to turn on seeing people's names and titles, but it was no longer split into Players, Pets, Mounts, and NPCs. She decided to change the setting to show names when targeted for People, Pets, and Mounts.

She hid HP bars unless they were below full health.

"How long does it take to die of dehydration?" she wondered aloud, tossing her Menu towards the chair where the church robe she'd been provided hung.

Chapter 2

Xander was not there when she'd finished bathing. Figuring he'd wandered off for the day, she took a seat on the couch she'd slept on and pondered what to do until he returned. She needed to find a way to log out but had no idea where to even start with that.

Feeling hungry, Astra opened her Inventory and pulled out one of the meals she'd crafted.

"Xander used to eat these pretty enthusiastically," she recalled. Whenever she had to log out, she'd always make sure he had plenty of meals in his inventory regardless of whether they were in town since he seemed to like her cooking so much. Whenever she came back, she'd find his supply either gone or diminished and supposed he'd eaten them. Unlike her, Xander didn't stop existing when she logged out.

VR had come a long way since its early days with bulky headsets that only tricked the eyes into believing you were in a digital landscape. The current technology interacted with the subconscious, turning off motor control the way sleep did and projecting the images straight into the wearer's brain. As a result, it really felt like you were there... to an extent.

Food tasted like a memory of eating something rather than a real sensation. Pain felt uncomfortable but didn't hurt more than an inconvenience. Pleasure got through better. As a result, X-rated VR games were popular. *Ashguard* was not one of those games, though it did have a high rating due to the graphic violence. Eating for her had only been a way to boost her stats temporarily, but Xander needed food and rest, or he fell behind and his health dipped.

She felt kind of bad about how she'd treated him. She wouldn't have taken a Porter if she hadn't needed the Inventory space. And only a Porter could put things for sale on the Market Board. Anyone could buy from it, but only a Porter could post items.

Taking a steaming plate of bacon and eggs from her Inventory, Astra bravely tried a bite.

Eyes widening, she sat back. "Cheese and crust! I'm a good cook!" *First time for everything!* She tucked into her breakfast.

When she finished the meal, the plate *poofed* out of existence the way these things always did in the game.

Astra collapsed back in the settee and stared up at the ceiling. She loved reading "stuck in a video game" stories, but those kinds of things happened to seventeen-year-olds, not thirty-four-year-old grocery store clerks.

It wasn't like my life was great, she thought. She could barely afford her apartment. Her supervisor at the store was an abusive jerk. He never gave her days off. Instead, he cut her hours and gave her split shifts. The customers were always the worst. She couldn't even afford to feed the local strays as a substitute for not having a pet. *Ashguard* had been the only bright spot in her life.

Now it was her life. At least until her body died or the power got cut on her apartment. Who knew when her time would be up, and here she was, sitting in Xander's church apartment, wasting the day away.

Something thumped against the door, and Astra turned her head to look.

Xander, juggling two plates and a stack of papers, managed to get the door open and slipped in, closing it with his foot. Coming to the table, he carefully set his burdens down.

"Oh. I already ate," Astra said, looking at the rather sad breakfast he'd brought.

"How?"

"Dude." Astra stared at him. "Crafting still works."

He didn't break eye contact as he slid the plates aside.

Breaking into a grin, Astra opened her inventory and set a plate of bacon and eggs out for him. Deciding not to waste the other two, she put them into her Inventory while he ate.

"I'm going to need materials to make more," Astra said, resting her arm along the back of the settee. Tapping her fingers, she stared into the distance in thought while she waited for him to finish. His plate *poofed*, and Xander sighed happily as he sat back. "What's all this?" she asked, pointing at the papers.

"Work," Xander said. "I usually do it elsewhere, but leaving you unattended..."

"I could explore the town?" Astra suggested.

"Absolutely not."

Ears folding down, Astra sighed. "Why?"

"You were seen by many people Resurrecting out of the Soul Stone. Word has spread that an Immortal has appeared."

Astra rolled her head back and groaned. "And Immortals are evil demons that eat children's souls," she concluded. "So as the stuck-up Divine Brother, it is your most sacred duty to make sure one doesn't just wander around buying supplies or something." Her tail thumped against the couch beside her.

"The very idea of you purchasing goods is terrifying. Fen was the currency Immortals used, and currently, they are only in circulation amongst the nobility," Xander pointed out.

"So, you're saying I've technically got no money." Astra melted over onto the cushions. "Ughhh! Why is life so hard?" she whined. Perking, she pushed onto her elbows. "I've got stuff I can sell! That shouldn't break the economy, right?"

He was shaking his head.

"If I only do it in small amounts?"

He still shook his head.

"I can sell high-quality things to the nobility? I'm sure they've got more money than they could spend in a lifetime."

Xander didn't look convinced.

"I'm not trying to break things, Xan. I'm bored. You can't keep me trapped here forever. What if I just went to the Southlands? Then you wouldn't have to deal with me at all."

"Except for when you get killed and reappear here," Xander pointed out.

Ears folding down, Astra laid her head on her arms, sprawling across the cushions on her stomach.

Xander remained unmoving and quiet. She didn't bother looking at him, hating how she was trapped by a society she knew nothing about with a guy who didn't seem to like talking.

"You may assist in the medical wing of the church," Xander said finally. "Would that suffice to alleviate your boredom?"

"I dunno. Would have to see the work involved."

"Then come." He stood, taking his stack of papers with him.

Astra cut a look at him. "Woof, woof," she muttered and got up.

* * *

"I recall the first time I cast Cure," Xander said as they walked. "You had just commanded that I cast it on you or myself should our health fall by ten percent." He glanced down, seeing a vague look in Astra's eyes. She did not remember this. "You promptly fell off a cliff," he added.

"Oh, yeah. Probably," she admitted with a grin.

"I was going to follow you down, but you ordered that I remain. You were within range, so I healed your wounds as ordered. However, I was promptly attacked by a Hedge Barker and slain."

Astra snickered. "Sounds about right."

Xander stopped and turned to face her. "Are you aware that dying hurts?" he asked.

"Yeah," Astra said and shrugged.

He sighed.

Turning away from her, he retook the lead. *I must keep in mind that she is Immortal,* he told himself. Perhaps seeing regular people in need of help would impress upon her the value of life. Reaching the medical wing of the church, Xander opened the door for her.

"This is triage," he said. "That door ahead is the waiting area. These doors are patient rooms."

Astra Diane nodded, looking at the directions he gestured.

"I will be in that office." Xander pointed at another door with a glass window. "Acolyte Heather," he called, catching sight of the young Elven maid as she was carrying a stack of supplies to a room.

"Yes, sir?" Heather asked and curtsied as she came to stand before him.

"Astra Diane will be shadowing you today. Show her your duties. If she attempts to do anything other than what you have shown her, inform me immediately." He saw Astra's ears flick down in annoyance from his peripheral.

Taking his papers to the office, he closed the door and got to work. For the last two hundred years, he'd been at the church. He didn't really have to work. He could've gone and crashed at any noble's house he wanted. Any of them would've been glad to have a Healer living with them, especially one that did healing for the low, low cost of remaining drunk.

However, he'd wanted something to keep his mind off Isabella.

What had started as a position at the medical wing had ended up with him teaching History and Monster Strategies at the academy. His current stack of papers was research papers on historical events. Honestly, he was utterly tired of reading about the same things repeatedly. He'd lived those "historical events," and they were mostly just painful memories to him. He needed a change.

It would only be a matter of time before the king and Holy Mouth came looking for Astra Diane. Maybe he should just take her to the Southlands and get lost?

* * *

Astra watched him go and shook her fist at his back before turning to Heather. "He acts like I don't have any common sense. I'm an adult. I don't need to be micromanaged."

"The Divine Brother is wise," Heather said in a small voice.

"Probably. But he's being a jerk right now," Astra stated. "All right, let's get this going. What're you carrying and where to?"

"Oh." Heather looked down at her bundle. "These are bandages. I was restocking the patient rooms."

"Then let's hop to it," Astra said.

Heather hesitated a moment more before nodding and turning to lead the way.

"Do you get a lot of patients here?" Astra asked as they entered an empty room. She watched where Heather began stocking the bandages, then wandered around the room, looking at the rest of the equipment: a bed, cupboards, and not much else...

"Sometimes," Heather said. "If there is a major incident in the city and the patients can make it here."

"Are there other hospitals in the city?" Astra asked. Not all the buildings had been accessible to Players, so she didn't know what other buildings existed in Aesir.

"No?" Heather paused, looking back at her.

"You don't know what a hospital is," Astra realized. "It's a medical facility, like this, but not attached to a church." She swung her finger around in a vague gesture to indicate the medical wing.

"Oh..." Heather said, her eyes wide. "No... there aren't enough Healers."

Tipping her head, Astra indicated she should go on.

"There are only thirty-six hundred known Healers," Heather said.

"Then who else works here? I saw other people walking around doing things out there," Astra gestured at the triage area.

"Medics," Heather said. "They rely on Alchemy to create cures. There are apothecaries who will sell alchemical mixtures for whatever people need."

Astra flicked her ears down, then back up, then down again. "I want to try something, but Xander will probably throw a fit." She sighed. "I'll talk to him about it later," she decided. "Do these Healers cap out at level one hundred?"

"No. Fifty."

That was some interesting information. A Skill traded Player to Player capped out at 100. Which left her wondering, what about a Player giving a Skill to an NPC? Would it be Unlocked or cap out at one hundred or fifty? Realizing that Heather was finished putting things away, Astra gestured towards the door. "Let's get back to work," she suggested.

"Oh! Right!" Heather exclaimed, looking flustered. She closed the cupboards and headed back into the triage area, leading Astra to a supply closet where she got another basket full of gauze and bandages.

Astra's attention was caught by a low health bar on a passing young man. He looked fine. He was assisting an old woman to walk toward one of the patient rooms. "She's fine," Astra said to Heather with a surreptitious point. "He's the one who needs help."

Heather looked flustered again. "I'll inform the medic," she said and handed Astra the basket of supplies. The honey blonde-haired Elven maid drew aside another man, who Astra assumed was the medic. After whispering in his ear, the man looked at Astra, then back at the pair of the old lady and young man that entered one of the patient rooms. The medic approached Astra.

"Could you tell what was wrong with him?" the Dracoid medic asked.

Astra shrugged. "His health was down forty percent," she said. "Didn't seem to be dropping lower, so probably not a lingering effect. Maybe an injury that isn't regenerating for some reason."

The medic nodded and went to the patient's room.

"Which room needs to be restocked next?" Astra asked Heather.

"This one," Heather said and led the way.

Taking the lead on putting things where they go, Astra sorted everything and then fronted it, pulling the items that were already in there to the front of the shelf and putting new behind it.

"Have you done this before?" Heather asked.

"I worked at a grocery store. Grocer? Market?" Astra said and stopped, folding her ears down. How much was she allowed to say about herself? Xander seemed to have taken it well enough, but then, he'd been in close proximity to Players. Heather had no experience with Players and what they were capable of.

"Such a humble profession for someone so powerful," Heather said after her initial expression of confusion cleared.

"Soul sucking," Astra said.

"How did you become Immortal then?" Heather asked.

"I'd rather not talk about that," Astra deflected.

"Oh."

Looking back at the girl, Astra found Heather clenching her hands together, looking down.

"Hey," Astra stepped closer, moving into the girl's line of sight by getting into her personal space. "Cheer up. You didn't upset me. Let's get to the next room."

"Right," Heather said and smiled a little. "You're very different from the way the Divine Brother described Immortals."

"Hm," Astra mused. "I liked taking on requests."

Heather tipped her head in thought. "He did say Immortals used to work for the Adventurers' Guild."

"Is there still an Adventurers' Guild?" Astra asked. When Heather nodded, she asked, "Who are the Adventurers now?"

"Brave people who wish to go out into the world, exploring, finding lost treasures, and assisting those who need help."

Astra nodded, following Heather as they went back to the supply closet. "Looks like you're running low on bandages," she noted.

"There's been a shortage lately," Heather explained and took the last of what was in the closet. "There was a monster attack, and we used a lot of our supplies on the City Guard."

Taking one of the bandages, Astra looked at it carefully. She didn't technically have a recipe for Bandages in her Tailor Skill, but she did have the ability to make this cloth. "Whose job is it to get more supplies?" she asked.

"Mine," Heather said. "I have to go into town next."

Astra grinned, holding up a hand. "Let's save you the trip." Pulling out her Menu, she searched through her Inventory and got the required materials to make linen cloth and proceeded to Craft six bolts of it before dropping them on the counter. This display caught the attention of everyone in the triage area.

"This is... such high-quality," Heather whispered, fingering the edge of the cloth. She turned wide eyes on Astra.

"My Tailor Skill is over five hundred," she said and shrugged. "I like Crafting. Shall we cut it up and turn it into bandages now?" Astra asked.

"R-right!" Heather breathed.

* * *

Reminded of the time by his rumbling stomach, Xander looked up from his paperwork and stretched. Only after remembering he was in the triage office did he recall that he'd left Astra Diane in the care of an acolyte for several hours and no one had come to inform him of trouble. He suspected something had gone wrong.

Getting up, he stepped out of the office to find Astra and Heather seated at the front desk, cutting and rolling bandages from fine linen.

Stepping closer, he pinned Astra with a glare. "I asked that you not—"

"Procuring new bandages was part of her duties," Astra interrupted, speaking without missing a snip of her scissors. "And I saved both time and money for the clinic, as well as alleviated the problem of low supplies due to a recent crisis. Patients will not be without proper medical equipment in the meantime."

"Please, sir, don't be angry at her," Heather said, hurrying to stand and bowed. "She has helped considerably."

Pinching the bridge of his nose, Xander sighed, feeling a headache building steadily.

"I was thinking, there are only three thousand Healers," Astra said. "I could make some Skill Scrolls. I'm limited to ten per day." She still hadn't bothered looking up from carefully cutting the cloth she was working on. "Not sure if they'd cap out the way they do when traded between p- Immortals. But I figured I'd ask before just doing it."

This cheeky little... Xander stared down at her, irritated by her determination to find loopholes in his rules. However... she was offering something valuable.

Astra paused in thought. "Though I probably shouldn't do it for free," she realized.

"We will discuss it later," Xander said, wanting to clear the subject from everyone's mind for the moment. "How many of these did you provide?" he asked, pointing at the bolts of fabric.

"Six," Astra said. "I figured that I'd just store whatever we don't need after we restock the closet."

At least she hadn't produced a large amount, but this fabric was higher quality than suitable for bandages. Then again, he wasn't sure she could make anything low quality. He'd seen her Skill levels. Lost in thought for a moment as he recalled how well she'd kept him even in the wilds, Xander had to remind himself that she'd thought him little more than an annoyance when he needed to rest or eat. *But the food was extremely good...*

"Sir," Heather said, drawing his attention. "I would like to have the Cure and Resurrection Skills."

"I've got some concerns," Astra said, putting down her scissors. "Heather said there's only three thousand Healers and their Skill caps at fifty. Where did they get the Skill from?"

"Not Immortals," Xander said, following her reasoning.

"Trading Skills between Immortals caps the Skill at one hundred," Astra said.

Xander lifted his hand to stop her. "You may test with one of your other Skills first," he said.

"All right," Astra said and pulled out her Menu. A few gestures later and she'd produced a Scroll. She handed it to Heather. "Tailor Craft Skill," she said.

Heather hesitated before taking the Scroll and opening it. In a flash, it disappeared from her hands.

Taking some basic materials out of her Inventory, Astra handed them to Heather. "Try crafting a basic spool of hemp with this."

"I'm..." she started to say, then Heather's eyes darted around as if reading something only she could see. The materials in her hands flashed into light and reappeared as a ball of twine. "Oh!"

Xander knew that feeling, having witnessed it himself every time Astra had given him a Skill. "There should be a number top right," he said.

"One of one hundred," Heather said.

A collective sigh went through the triage from the other medics present. They too had hoped that an Immortal would be able to impart Uncapped Skills.

"Do you still want Cure and Resurrect?" Astra asked. "They'll cap at one hundred too."

Heather set the ball of twine down. "Yes! Please!"

Admittedly, it was still better than any other Healer aside from Xander himself. He'd been the one to give most of those Cure and Resurrect Skills out and been disappointed that they capped at fifty. Immortals were the only ones capable of creating Uncapped Skills.

Astra repeated her process, handing Heather two more Scrolls, which she immediately consumed.

"Thank you!" the acolyte breathed and bowed to Astra, then to Xander.

* * *

Following Xander, Astra watched his hair sway against his back. *This view of him is pretty nice too*, she mused. He had a slender build but broad shoulders. "Did you even want to be a Healer?" she asked, thinking that he might have made a good swordsman too.

He glanced back at her. "It is a fine Class," he said.

"But did you want to be a Healer?" she insisted.

"I had gone into the guild expecting to become a

Mage or Warrior," he admitted finally. Opening a door, he gestured for her to go through.

Astra breathed in the scent of fresh air and grass. Tail flicking in excitement, she hurried out into the garden and went to the center to drop into the grass, rolling in it. Stretching her arms over her head she flopped out full eagle and smiled.

Xander stared down at her with his impassive expression for a long moment before he gracefully folded to sit in the grass beside her. His gaze was fixed on the far wall.

Sitting up, she opened her Inventory and pulled out some lunch for them both, placing the bowl of Ramen into his hands when she didn't immediately get a reaction.

Dropping his gaze to the food, Xander took it. "Thank you," he said, voice barely audible. "Why did you choose me?" he asked.

"I don't think you'll like the answer," Astra said honestly.

He sighed. He couldn't look at her and instead focused his gaze on his food. For a moment, they both ate silently. The food seemed to calm his nerves, at least.

"I was an orphan," he said. "I'd just come of age when the Immortals first appeared. At first, we all believed they were benevolent... That they meant well. The Adventurers' Guild handled requests and sent them out to do things we couldn't. Such as handling monsters that were far too powerful for us to deal with on our own. I worked in an item shop at that time, but the shop couldn't compete with the potions and items Immortals were bringing in and Crafting. I was released from the contract."

Astra cringed. "Getting fired sucks," she agreed, "Especially when you've got nowhere else to go. Been there. Done that."

Her words caught his attention and he looked at her with a slightly lifted brow.

"My mom was an alcoholic; dad ran off with some floozie when I was six. I worked at a convenience store when I was sixteen." Astra took a breath and let it out. "That's where I got..." She stopped. She couldn't even say it. Her hands tightened on the bowl. "Anyway. After a year, the boss got tired of me and tossed me out, but by then, Mom had shacked up with some other jerk and didn't want me around. I got a membership at a gym and lived in their bathroom for a year before getting a job at the grocery store."

She forced herself to smile and looked up at him— only to be confronted by his expression of utter sorrow. "H-hey, d-don't do that!" She shuffled to turn her back on him and focused on eating her ramen. "Get back to your story," she muttered.

Xander remained quiet for a moment and said, "I signed up for the Immortal Assistant project. They promised adventure and the opportunity to obtain Unlocked Skills. They did not mention that we would be compelled to obey orders and unable to speak to you."

"Compelled?" Astra asked, looking back over her shoulder at him, ears folded down.

"At least you did not use me the way other Immortals used their assistants," Xander said.

"I still got you killed a few times," Astra said. "Because I wasn't paying attention. So... sorry about that. For what it's worth. But I couldn't understand you. All I ever got were notifications that you were hungry or tired."

Silence fell between them. Xander's bowl *poofed* away, but Astra couldn't finish hers.

"I suspect," Xander said, "You chose me because I was nice to look at?"

The hint of amusement in his voice made her look up. "It took me a whole week to find someone up to my standards," Astra retorted.

"I feel honored." He gave the slightest of bows.

* * *

Xander let the silence sit for a while and instead looked up at the cloudless sky. That had been a... deeply uncomfortable conversation for the both of them. Even though he'd lived hundreds of years, the memory of that time still stung, but hearing that she, an Immortal, had gone through similar experiences was shocking. From her tone, he suspected she was far younger than he.

"How old are you?" he asked.

"Thirty-four," Astra answered without hesitation.

"Is this what you always looked like?" Xander asked.

"Well, my face, kinda. But I always hated being the 'Tall Girl' and never getting enough to eat made me pretty flat. So, when I got the chance to make my own body, this was what I chose." Astra looked up at him. She'd found her composure and smiled. "If you could remake yourself, what would you look like?"

Xander stared at her in thought. "I'm not sure," he admitted.

She burst out laughing. "Of course. A face like yours, who would change it?" She pushed his shoulder and continued giggling.

He stared down at her, watching as she finished off her lunch and the bowl *poofed* away. *Thirty-four,* he mused. She'd had a tough life. No wonder she had come to Ashguard to be an Immortal. "Why did you choose Healer?" he asked.

Leaning back on her hands, she shook her hair back from her shoulders and smiled at him. "I like helping people. I didn't realize that it would be such an underappreciated Class. Or that I'd get harassed constantly for Skill Scrolls by other Players. Made getting through dungeons difficult when the Warriors would just charge ahead and gather the entire area's monsters then get mad at me when they died. Like I can't help it if they're morons."

"Dungeons? You never took me into those places," Xander observed.

"Wasn't allowed to," Astra said. "Makes me wonder what it was preventing you from talking to me... what exactly runs this place." She tipped her head slightly. "I accessed Ashguard through my headset... So, what happened to my body? How is it five hundred years later? Time here runs faster, so twelve hours at home was a full day and night cycle here. Five hundred years is..."

"Two hundred and fifty," Xander supplied. "Approximately. It hasn't been exactly five hundred since the Immortals disappeared."

"What happened with that?" she asked. She didn't look like she fully believed his math. "Maybe everyone just got kicked off for the update?"

He looked away. "Your health suddenly depleted and you did not come back," Xander said, "A few days later, all Immortals were simply gone."

"Sounds disconcerting," Astra said.

"It was. After years of pointless battles in public spaces, the central square was simply empty. Taverns... the Guild Hall. We all waited for the Immortals to return. When years passed and you did not, the Cursed Ones began fighting among each other."

"Cursed Ones?" she asked, tipping her head to look at him, chin resting against her shoulder.

"Your assistants. We discovered that while we could die of wounds, we did not age."

Her ears flicked down, pupils shrinking as the repercussions of that hit her.

"It was another side effect of the Pact we made with the Immortals. No one knew until assistants who should have visibly grown old did not," Xander explained. "Several assistants with little else to do with the Skills they had acquired, began fighting over the Vanaheim throne. That battle lasted for fifty years. Others retreated from society, taking over the towns Immortals had created near the border of the Southlands. Still, others chose to take up adventuring since there were still monsters that required extermination that normal citizens could not hope to face."

"What about you?" Astra asked.

"For a time, I adventured, working with a few others to take count of the death toll from the Plague. Time passed, and the few Healers with Unlocked Skills died one by one. Now, only I remain." That was not exactly how it had happened, but Astra Diane did not need to know anything about Isabella, or Baldur. "I had been away from the Cursed City for too long and did not find any friends among those who lived there. Instead, I chose to return to Aesir. Vanaheim seemed too unstable and given the reputation Cursed Ones had there, I decided to avoid it, despite having been born there. I now teach monster extermination tactics and history at the Academy and work with the clinic at the church. I tried to increase the number of Healers, but my Skill Scrolls cap at level fifty."

Astra covered his hand, leaning in. "Don't compare yourself to Immortals," she said, "We're cheating. I'm sure of it. What you've achieved, you did on your own power."

Unexpectedly touched by her encouragement, Xander felt his heart skip. Pulling his hand away, he set his shoulders. "Aesir's royalty wishes to go to war with Vanaheim," he said. "The Holy Mouth will undoubtedly speak to you as soon as she gets the opportunity."

She waited for him to finish, the weight of her silence pressing on him.

"I do not wish to return to battle," he said. "I have refused... However, I cannot control your actions."

Her ears flicked down. "What's the fight even about?"

"A Cursed One named Johnas took the throne some ten years ago. He has steadily raised taxes on imports and exports to Vanaheim. Aesir's merchants have found it most vexing. They have pressured King James to do something. I have been harassed and begged on multiple occasions."

"Then it's not my problem," Astra said. "And I'm not going to drag you into it when you're happy in your retirement." She pulled her knees against her chest and wrapped her arms around them. "If I leave, I'll probably just go back to the Southlands."

"That still leaves the problem of other Immortals," Xander reminded. "You may decline, but others may not be so kind as to keep to themselves."

Astra sighed. "Yeah. A lot of the Players I knew would jump at the chance to get involved in a war, regardless of what it was about." She set her chin on her knees, ears twitching as thoughts went through her mind at high speed. "I doubt they'd listen to me if I asked them to stay out of it. The best answer is to get rid of us entirely. But where to start on that..."

"I have been giving the matter some considerable thought. The Soul Stones are what allows Immortals to reappear after death."

"Yeah. Getting rid of them," Astra muttered. Her ears had slanted back slightly. "But they've been at the center of Mage battles and not taken a scratch." Her ears flattened entirely as she glared into the distance. "That jerk camped the Soul Stone for hours. I lost fifteen stat points that day."

"Pardon?" Xander asked.

"Before we met," Astra said with a flick of her fingers. "Mage named Horhay kept targeting the Nifelheim Soul Stone Plaza with Fire Bombs and killing everyone there. Every time someone respawned, he'd do it again. Thankfully a Warrior with higher levels showed up and shanked him. Chased his butt around town for a while, but not nearly enough."

"Perhaps investigating what the Soul Stones are will lead to what powers them?" Xander suggested.

"Probably," Astra said. "I'll help however I can... Xander... it's been a while since I couldn't log out. The longer I leave my body just... laying there... something could happen. I need to log out and I don't know how."

"Perhaps the library will have answers?" Xander suggested. "I will take you there." He got to his feet and offered his hand to help her up.

* * *

As soon as Xander left her, Astra's ears folded down.

"I never finished high school," she said as she stared at the massive number of books. Endless shelf after shelf of the church's library, stacked two stories high and the length of a soccer field. "What the heck does he expect me to do here?" At least he'd decided it was safe to leave her to her own devices and hadn't assigned a babysitter. She rather wished she had one, though.

The last time she'd been in a library was middle school. She'd been assigned a paper on the oxygen cycle or something. She'd failed it.

It wasn't that she didn't like reading, either. She just... struggled with it.

Astra started walking down the central aisle, glancing left and right as she found open spaces with tables. There were people at some of the tables, buried in stacks of books, taking notes. She [Examined] them out of curiosity.

[Brother Kyle] was a Human male with brown hair... [Sister Lillie] was a blue Dracoid... [Hugh, Professor of History] was a redheaded Giant...

Astra stopped and backed up. Ahh! Perfect!

"Pardon," an old voice, sounding a little out of breath, said.

Stopping her intended path to harass the professor, Astra turned to find a Dracoid so old their coloring had faded to grey. [Grestra, The Holy Mouth] was addressing her. Ears dropping down, then up again, she turned to face the woman. "Greetings, Holy One. Is there something I can help you with?"

The Dracoid smiled, sharp teeth poking from her mouth. "Might I have a moment of your time, Adventurer?"

Too late, Astra noticed the Dracoid had put an arm around her shoulders and turned her away from the professor she'd wanted to talk to. Ears folding down, Astra had no choice but to be led away.

The Holy Mouth continued, "Our country is suffering—"

"Mnn," Astra said. "Xander said something about this. I'm going to save you some time and let you know I think he's right."

The Holy Mouth's fingers tightened on her shoulder. "He is unaware of the full picture."

"Look... I don't think I'd even be that much help," Astra said. "I'm Healer Class. I don't have any offensive Skills except Raise Undead..."

"That is precisely why we require your assistance," the Dracoid said. She had already drawn Astra back towards the door to the library and out into the hall. "There are only so many Healers left in the world."

"Something like three thousand," Astra said. "Look, I'm not doing anything without compensation."

"Of course, we will compensate you."

Astra was highly uncomfortable with this little chat and where she was being taken. She'd never been this far into the church building before. Her exploits had always ended at the sanctuary to get Holy Water for her Death Penalty. The building itself was incredibly large. She glanced to the right as they passed by windows that looked into the courtyard she and Xander had just had lunch in. Her ears flicked down, tail swaying in agitation.

"I heard that you gave Acolyte Heather a Skill Scroll this morning," the Dracoid said.

"Um. Yeah. That was a gift. Because I wanted to," Astra said, unable to break away.

"Her new Skills cap at one hundred. That's rather kind of you. She has wanted to be a Healer for years. We have been researching how to surpass the level fifty limit of the Scrolls Xander can create."

"Hmm... and that has what to do with me?" Astra asked.

"We will need people capable of using Cure and Resurrect if we want to avoid loss of life. But beyond that, people who are capable of creating textiles and equipment." The Holy Mouth opened a door, leading Astra into an office wherein a Human man and a Giant sat in chairs near a fancy desk.

Astra [Examined] them. [Prince Rufus el Aesir] was a young Human man with blond hair and blue eyes. He had an arrogant smile. [Chancellor Jotun] was the Giant with a long mane of greying black hair and opulent jewels on the crushed velvet doublet he wore. Astra's gaze flicked down to his doublet; [Crushed Velvet Doublet, Level 50]. Figuring she'd better be polite, she did something like a bow. "Your Highness, Chancellor," she greeted.

Rufus and Jotun smiled, the Chancellor speaking before the prince could. "A well-informed woman, I see."

Astra considered telling them that she could see their names and titles, then decided not to. Instead, she put on a customer service smile and stood, waiting for them to get to the part where they tried to bend her over and take her for everything she had.

Rufus stood and offered his hands out. "It is well and truly an honor to meet an Immortal," he said, taking her hands. Clasping them near his chest, he bowed.

Unable to stop her ears from flicking down in distress, Astra waited for the man to let her go and stepped back to put some distance between them again. Unsure of what to say, she remained silent.

"Please, Honored Immortal, sit," the Holy Mouth said, gesturing at one of the remaining seats. "We should discuss compensation for your services." The Dracoid gave Astra no room to say no and pulled her into the chair.

Trapped, she wrapped her tail into her lap and picked at the fur, petting it to soothe herself.

"What Skills do you have, My Lady Immortal?" Jotun asked, leaning forward. The chair he sat in creaked slightly.

"She is Healer Class," the Holy Mouth said, handing out cups of tea around the room.

Astra took the cup and stared into it, unsure if she should drink or not.

"Her Tailor Craft Skill is impressive," the Holy Mouth said. "Do you possess other Craft Skills?"

"Yeah," Astra said. "Blacksmith, Alchemist, Arborist,

Farmer, Miner, and Hunter."

"Are these sufficiently leveled that you could provide Skill Scrolls?" Jotun asked.

Astra glanced up, finding Rufus smiling charmingly at her. Good cop, bad cop? Or was it Interrogator and Honey Pot? Rufus was pretty but fell way short in comparison to Xander, and she still wouldn't have bought what he was trying to sell. "Yes," Astra said, lifting her ears as she found confidence.

This situation was in her favor. She had all the cards. Now she just needed to think of an outrageous price for her help.

* * *

Entering his office, Xander wondered if it was really all right to leave Astra alone in the Library. He knew that Rufus and the Chancellor were waiting in the Holy Mouth's office, but he had prepared Astra for the encounter as best he could. She seemed to agree with Xander's sentiments. It was up to her whether she agreed to help them or not. Pulling the papers from his Inventory, he set them on his desk and sighed. He'd gotten through grading half of them, but concentrating on research papers...

"They say sighing makes you shorter and considering you're already fairly short for an Elf..."

Turning, Xander found Kayson leaning against the wall behind the door. The Human man was another Cursed One. He fell somewhere between remaining in public and hiding from the populace. His information guild knew everything about everything. If they didn't know, they would find out. Xander had made use of them a few times, which was how he'd come to know Kayson. Their shared experience of feeling their Immortal die had made them something closer than acquaintances.

"Is there something you want?" Xander asked, irritated. "And take off those ridiculous glasses."

"I got them from my Immortal," Kayson said and smiled. He did take the round lenses sunshades off and folded the earpieces with his other hand, striding forward in a smug strut. "Speaking of Immortals... I heard a little rumor that you've been hiding one."

"Not hiding," Xander said, separating out the papers he'd graded from those he hadn't read yet. Anything to not look at Kayson.

Kayson leaned on the edge of the desk next to him. "Then I may speak to her freely?"

"No." Slapping his papers down, Xander turned to look at the man. "There is no reason for you to do so."

A grin spread across his mouth as the handsome Human said, "So it's true she can hear us. The others were betting that she would be like the Immortals before; unable to respond to anything we said outside the script."

Xander hated dealing with this man. No matter what was said, he got information out of it, somehow. Absolutely infuriating. Straightening, Xander decided to give him a cold glare instead of saying anything else. If Kayson got bored, perhaps he'd go away. By now, Astra would be locked in the Holy Mouth's office and out of the man's reach.

Kayson had one last thing to impart before he left. "I've been offered a lot of money to arrange a meeting between her and Johnas. He's keen on becoming an assistant again."

"Why?"

"Why else?" Kayson replied with a lift of his hands. "Immortals can impart Unlocked Skills, of course."

"She only has Healer Class Skills," Xander said.

"But if she were to be led to other Skill Masters, she would be able to get more," Kayson said. "And thanks for confirming that you are her current assistant. In honor of our longstanding friendship, I'll give you the opportunity to buy my silence. For a time."

"You would start a bloodbath," Xander said, cold dread seeping through his core. "There's no guarantee she will be willing to make a Pact with anyone else."

"A little bird told me you killed her. If a weak Healer can kill her, then what chance does she have against anyone else? She'll break eventually. Time's up." Kayson flipped his glasses open and slipped them back on. "See you later, Xan."

* * *

The door to the hall rattled. Astra glanced towards it, as did the others.

For a second, nothing. Then the frame broke as the door slammed back on its hinges. Xander caught his balance and glanced around the room, expression grim.

Striding in, he grabbed her wrist and pulled her to her feet. Her grip on the teacup slipped, but she was already out the door by the time it hit the floor. "Xan!" she objected, trying to pull free. "Xan—stop!"

"We need to leave now," he said firmly. He stopped suddenly and turned to face her. "You and I are in a great amount of danger. We must get you leveled up and quickly."

Astra stared up at him. He smelled terrified. His expression was as impassive as usual, but his hand on her wrist was trembling.

The Holy Mouth, Rufus, and Jotun were coming down the hall towards them, objecting loudly to Xander's interruption.

Deciding to trust him, Astra nodded, reached into her pocket, and pulled out her Menu. Going to her teleport list, she selected the Soul Stone Shard she'd dropped just before she died in the Southlands and grabbed Xander's wrist.

A Teleport circle opened beneath her feet, spreading out with rays of light spiking upwards. In seconds, it snapped closed, taking them with it.

When the greenery of the Southlands unfolded around them, Xander dropped to a knee and breathed heavily, arm still in Astra's grip. That was apparently something that hadn't changed with him. He'd always gotten ill whenever she Teleported them to places.

"Okay. Explain now? We're on the west edge of the Dark Mountains. That should be far enough away, right?"

Xander nodded, his head still bowed, the silver curtain of hair hiding his face. He took a moment longer to find his composure and stood. "Teleporting always makes me... nauseous," he admitted. Pushing his hair back from his face, he looked down at her. "Word has spread that an Immortal has returned. The Cursed One Johnas has paid the information guild run by Kayson to take you to him."

"So?" Astra asked as she looked through her inventory for her armor and weapon. She then went hunting for something for Xander.

"They will want you to make a Pact with them in order to have access to Unlocked Skills—" He paused when his clothes exploded in sparks, replaced by the leathers she'd selected.

"But I already have a Porter," Astra said.

"Exactly," Xander said. "They would kill me, then begin slaughtering each other."

Her ears folded down. "That's a problem for you."

"And you. They know you are lower level than they are. They will kill you as many times as it takes to force you to do as they wish."

Tail stilling, Astra stared up at him. "That sounds like a big problem," she admitted. "The only way to protect ourselves would be to start leveling up our Skills."

Xander nodded.

Looking away, Astra breathed in, then out deliberately. "So much for your peaceful retirement." Turning to face him again, she asked, "What about investigating the Soul Stones? There's going to be no end to this problem as long as I'm here..."

"Unless there are other Immortals," Xander said, his hands busy pulling his hair back and tying it into a high tail. "In which case, their attention will be diverted for the time being. For now, should you die, allow me to Resurrect you."

Astra nodded, feeling her cheeks grow hot at the idea of getting rescued by her Porter.

Chapter 3

The rocky terrain made traveling at a pace difficult. Forested mountains surrounded them, littered with granite boulders and fallen trees meant there were no clear paths. Astra had taken the lead but honestly had no idea where to go. She needed to level, which meant that she would need to find enemies to fight. Which Skill should she level, though? Raise Undead was high already.

"Let's camp for the night," Xander said. There was still plenty of daylight left.

She looked back at him, finding him standing braced against a tree branch, one foot on a fallen log she'd hopped over.

Ears falling, Astra said, "Sorry, didn't know you were tired." Now that she'd stopped, Astra realized that she was tired, legs trembling and back sweaty beneath her leather armor. She'd picked out her second-best armor since her best set was ruined by the Razor Boar.

She had let go of the notion that all this was an update to *Ashguard*. If it was, they'd changed everything about the game and made it a single player. Things were too real; from sweat sticking her shirt to her skin to the bugs annoying her ears. Then, there was the fact that she still couldn't log out. While the game had been out for four years, she didn't think the developers would change everything like that without warning. That only left the option that she was actually in Ashguard and it was a real world, not a game at all.

"I'm not, but it will be too dark to make a proper camp if we wait much longer," Xander said.

"Right..." Feeling awkward, Astra turned to look around the area. It wasn't very clear, but she supposed it would do? She'd never been in charge of making the camps since she had never been the one who needed them.

"Clear the leaves from here," Xander directed, pointing with a stick he'd picked up. "We'll put the fire there."

"Oh. Okay." Glad to have something useful to do, she pulled out her farming rake and got started. Shortly, she had the whole area down to the dirt, the leaves piled on one side. It had been clearer than she'd thought, and pulling the small shrubs wasn't difficult. Xander dropped a load of sticks into the center and started arranging them.

It wasn't like Astra needed a fire in order to feed them, though. Sitting down across the way, she watched him until he dropped his hands to his lap.

"Don't have anything to start it with, do you?" she asked coyly.

"I fear not," he said.

Reaching out, Astra said, "[Fire Bullet]," and shot the spark into the dirt at the center of the pyramid of sticks. The explosion of flame roared forth and she rubbed her eyebrows, checking that she still had them.

Xander had his eyes squeezed shut. He breathed out his nose. "Your mastery of that will increase to the point where you won't be able to do that," he said.

"Okay, Mom." Astra opened her Inventory to find some food. Pulling out two meals, she offered him his choice. He chose the Hearty Stew, leaving her with the Steak and Potatoes. "Wandering in circles wont get us anywhere," she said.

"We aren't wandering. We are hunting for monsters."

"I was exploring the Southlands because I heard a rumor about another Soul Stone," Astra said. "Ruins on the edge of a lake." Spearing a piece of potato with her fork, she ate it. "I was sure it was an area they were going to open as an expansion."

"I cannot understand what you are talking about," Xander said honestly, "Expansion?"

"Oh boy. Um. So... Ah! Like if you're playing Nines. But then someone comes up with some new cards for it. They fit into the original game, but they're new," Astra explained. "An expansion. I thought that they might open a new city to keep things fresh and Players interested in coming to Ashguard."

Xander shook his head, although she could tell he understood now. "I've never heard of any lakeside ruins. However, I was not a history scholar." He ate a few more bites of his stew before saying, "We could continue searching for it if that pleases you."

Something about the way he said it made her feel a little sad. Before, when she'd been playing by herself, the long stretches of not talking to anyone hadn't mattered. Even when she'd had Xander following behind her, she had considered herself alone. Now that he could hold a conversation with her... it seemed so wrong to have him subservient to her.

"You're a person," she said, "Not my slave."

He looked across the fire at her. She didn't look up from playing with her food.

"I am glad to hear you think that way," Xander said.

"We should have a watch or something," she said. "In case of monsters attack while we're asleep."

"How long does your Raise Undead last?" Xander asked instead.

"Uh... at this point, practically until they're defeated," Astra answered.

"Then Raise Undead and command them to attack anything that comes near us."

She lifted her head. "Will that work?"

"Yes, I've done it on the road in order to get occasional naps," Xander said.

"Okay. [Raise Undead]." She held her hand out. All at once, a shuffling in the woods rustled the leaves and undergrowth as magically created Undead rose from the earth. They wandered away from the small camp, the tiny army creating a buffer between the pair of Healers and anything that could cause them harm.

Astra made herself finish dinner. Her plate *poofed* and shortly later, Xander's did too. Astra curled on her side on the ground, pulling her tail up around her shins to keep them warm. It was getting chilly.

"Do you have a cloak?" Xander asked.

"Oh." Astra sat up, pulling her Menu from her pocket to look through her Inventory. "Would be convenient if you could access mine the way I do yours," she mused. Finding some furs, Astra Crafted them into Fur Rugs and tossed them on the ground, followed by some Wool Blankets. "There, that should do it."

Xander stood, coming to sit next to her. "At least traveling with you is always done in luxury."

84

The fire had gone out during the night.

Astra had ended up snuggling against him, both of them wrapped in Xander's blanket. He'd woken with her cuddled against him in the past, but this time was different. He knew she had actually fallen asleep. However, knowing she was Felis, he wondered if his waking up had woken her up, something he didn't want to do right away.

She had her head on his chest, his arm had ended up around her shoulders. It had been a very long time since he'd slept with anyone. Having someone gently breathing beside him was... nice. The fact that it was an Immortal... his Immortal... the one he'd wanted to hold for a very long time. It was a difficult thing to admit to himself.

He'd been lonely for the longest time but pushed everyone away. The few lovers he'd had were always temporary. After all, they would grow old and die. Then there was the fact that he was insufferably depressed and drunk for a lot of that time. Then there was Isabella... He still couldn't quite forgive her, even though seeing Astra again made him realize why Isabella had always complained that she felt like a replacement for something.

Xander's fingers tightened on Astra's shoulder involuntarily.

They needed to get up.

Astra sat up, tearing the blanket off him in her movement. Her face was so flushed he could practically feel the heat radiating off her cheeks. "I'm... gonna go—" she sputtered, unable to fully explain where she was going or why. She just got up and hurried off into the trees, leaving him by himself.

Propping himself up on one elbow, he gazed after her

for a second, then got up. He shook out the blankets and rugs, folded them, and stuck them in his Inventory.

Composure found, Astra returned, wiping her hands through her short hair. "Okay, so... We'll keep heading west. I smell running water that way. If we follow that downstream, we will eventually get to a lake. Probably."

Xander nodded. "Lead the way, then." She didn't want to talk about sleeping on him, then fine, he wouldn't bring it up. It wasn't as if he'd minded, though...

* * *

Astra could not keep her tail from thrashing in embarrassment. Xander hadn't said anything, and she couldn't tell what he was thinking. His cold expression remained the same as usual. Those icy eyes had stared up at her upon waking with the same passionless dismissal they held now as he ate breakfast.

Her ears folded briefly. "There is a time limit to my Raise Undead," she said. "They just despawned."

Xander nodded.

Finished eating, Astra stood and looked down at the remains of the fire. "[Ice Bullet]," she said, making sure it was completely out. The pile of ash froze over instantly.

"Should probably make a fire starter set," Xander said as he dusted his pants off. He adjusted his hair before looking at her. "Later," he added.

Ears flicking down, Astra nodded and forced her ears back up. Having ears and a tail made her emotions so readable, she realized. Back when she'd been simply Human, she could Resting Witch Face or Customer Service

Smile her way through any situation. But now, her body just did whatever, it seemed. Reaching back, she itched her tail, then pulled it around to pick some leaves out of the hair and smoothed it down. She'd chosen a fluffy tail when she'd created her character. Now she was regretting that as she came out with a hand full of loose hair. Dusting her hands, wiped the remaining white strands on her pant legs. Maybe she could Craft a comb while she was at it?

Turning, she sniffed the air, located the direction of the stream, and started walking.

Xander fell in behind her, although he walked closer than he used to when he was simply her Porter. She felt her tail bump him every now and then.

"Monster ahead," he said.

Astra sniffed the air. Indeed, there was something stinky mixed with the smell of running water. How had he noticed it before she did?

"[Shelter]," Xander cast on her.

The shield enveloped her like a second skin. She could tell it was a much higher level than she was capable of casting. "[Shelter]," she cast on him, just to get the point towards a level. Ranging ahead, Astra came upon a Razor Boar. It had blood on its sharp tusks and a scar across its eye. "That's the jerk that killed me the other day," she recognized. Well, it was payback time. It hadn't noticed them; it was busy drinking at the stream. Astra climbed a tree to get some higher ground and started her barrage of Elemental Mastery.

Xander had found a safe place to watch some distance away, keeping an eye out for any other monsters while Astra whittled the Boar down practically one point at a time.

"Ugh, this is going to take forever," she complained while the Boar slashed and bashed at the tree she sat in. The tree shook with its infuriated attacks.

"Keep at it," Xander said.

Casting a glare at him, she shot an Ice Bullet in his direction. It bounced off the Shelter she'd cast, as she knew it would. Turning back to the Razor Boar, she took aim and started attacking again.

By the time she killed it, she'd leveled Elemental Mastery fifteen times, bringing it to just under level fifty. Climbing down from the tree, she equipped her Hunting Knife to make use of the Boar's meat and other materials.

Xander came to stand beside her as she worked, looking downstream with an unreadable expression. He sure was pretty to look at. His sharp features set in a slender face, framed by silver hair were the essence of an ice sculpture. A breeze pulled strands of that hair, tickling the edge of his jaw. He turned to look down at her. "Done?"

"Oh. Yeah."

Feeling herself blushing again, Astra switched her Hunting Knife back to her Healer Focus and started walking, heading downstream.

"Tell me about your world?" Xander asked.

"Uhm. Not sure where to start," Astra said. "We had more technology and no magic. We didn't use Skills like you do here. We didn't have Inventory." She glanced back to see his puzzled expression.

"If you did not have magic, how did Immortals appear in this world?"

Astra had to look back at the trail she was following

to keep her footing. "We had a technology called Virtual Reality. It was like a crown we put on that would interact with our brains and make our brains believe we were somewhere else while our bodies may as well have been asleep."

"How is this not magic?" Xander asked.

"Because it was a device with many little parts and pieces in it that directed electricity to make things happen," Astra said. "It was something that got put together in a factory and normal people could buy. Like buying a carrot. You could just buy this thing. It was how we interacted with a lot of stuff, not just Ashguard. There were other games people played using it. People taught classes from anywhere in the world for everything and everything."

"If there were other games..." Xander said, "What made you choose to come to Ashguard?"

Astra thought about it for a time. "I joined when it was still kinda new." She looked up at the trees, noticing the scent of rain in the air. "Weather's changing," she said.

"Let's move a bit away from the stream."

Adjusting course, she continued speaking, "I'd heard that you could practically do anything you wanted in Ashguard. Past picking one of the three Classes, you could get Skills outside of your class and be a Holy Knight, or Death Knight and the Crafting system let you make whatever you felt like making. There seemed to be a lot of options for a relatively small game and the graphics weren't a bunch of repeated pictures. It was like visiting a real alien world." She understood why now. It had always been another world.

She glanced back. Xander's brows were creased. He

may not have understood most of what she said. "Uhm... Let me try again?" she offered and started from a more basic point of what "graphics" were and how other games functioned.

"You've read books, right? Well, games like this are usually like books. Every Player goes through the story the same way, taking the role of the main character."

"You said you came here for the story," Xander said.

"Yeah. The story that they sold us was that we were chosen by the gods to serve as champions of the people. We had the power to start or end wars, create or destroy kingdoms, and break the limits of the Skills. Ashguard didn't get very popular. Mostly because there wasn't a set story and by several months in, a lot of Players had ruined stuff and it was obvious that the game itself couldn't police us. So other Players started making guilds to keep Player abuse to an acceptable level.

"But of course, when one bunch sets some rules, another bunch has to go out of their way to break them and it just escalates. Then there are the jerks who join the police just so they can lord it over everyone else and break the rules themselves. And no one had actually ever agreed on the rules. At its peak, there were a hundred thousand Players, but that fell to a couple thousand after the first year."

She pursed her lips. "Wish I knew why everyone just up and left for five hundred years."

* * *

Unable to contain his fury at the audacity of these Immortals, Xander fought to remain silent. Chosen by the gods? Of all the arrogance... These people came from another world, thought it was all a game, destroyed countless lives, and justified it how?

Astra stopped and turned to face him. "Is something wrong?" she asked, looking genuinely confused.

He'd intended to stay silent... intended to brush it off as nothing.

But then she smiled.

"I am astounded by the arrogance of your people," Xander said. "That you would transport yourselves to our world without knowing a single thing about us and claim to be chosen by the gods! Have you any idea what the gods even represent to us?"

Astra's ears folded down. "I—"

He cut her off. "Even if you had been chosen by the gods, your people's behavior was a disgrace to their name. You came here with the sole purpose of destroying or building our world to your liking, for your own entertainment! Simply because we could not fight back!"

"You signed up to be a Porter!" Astra shouted, finding her voice.

"Because I saw no other option that would keep me alive!" Xander shouted. "The first time I died was when I stepped out of the Guild Hall with you!"

"So, it's all my fault?" she demanded. "I'm to blame for all Players?!"

"Your fault is in participating in the system—"

"Then why don't you leave?" she demanded. "You're free to! Nothing is making you follow me around! Here—

I'll send you back to Aesir!" Astra pulled out her Menu.

Snatching it from her hand, Xander struggled to get his emotions under control.

"Then send yourself back," Astra said and turned away, stalking off into the woods.

Pinching the bridge of his nose as he allowed his blood to cool, Xander focused on breathing.

The sky opened up in a sudden downpour that almost immediately drenched him. Shoving the Menu into his pocket, Xander started walking, following his Directional Sense of where Astra was. He knew he wasn't wrong in being angry. But that didn't make him right either. It was just... now that he had the opportunity to confront an Immortal for all the things they'd done, rationality had simply left him.

Astra hadn't gone into villages and slaughtered everyone. She'd mostly spent her time exploring and crafting, taking on requests that weren't out of her way. In most regards, she had been one of the better Immortals. He did recall her casting Cure on people they passed with no benefit to her...

The problem was the blame. Where did hers start and end? What use was it to blame her now? His family had been dead long before the Immortals came to the world. Others were made orphans by the Immortals, though five hundred years had passed, and the only ones left alive to remember that time was the couple hundred Cursed Ones. Who was he angry for?

Himself, Xander decided. He could only be angry for himself. Everyone else's anger was their own burden to carry and most of them were dead. The only thing he could do now was get her to acknowledge the things she'd personally done.

Xander scowled at the soggy path as his boots splashed through the mud. She'd already said she couldn't change the past, just work towards being better in the future. "Gods," he muttered. He was going to have to apologize. For better or worse, he was stuck with her, and while he had her Menu, she couldn't perform a lot of tasks. Did she really expect to get far without it?

On that thought, how was she moving so swiftly?

Opening the Menu, he carefully went through it, finding her Skills. She did have Cavalry and Summoning. Perhaps she'd used one of those?

He sighed. "Really? How petty," he muttered. He would catch up with her eventually.

Her health took a hit. Seconds later, she had none.

She was still getting further away despite being dead.

Xander shoved the Menu into his pocket and started jogging.

* * *

Astra used the back of her hand to wipe her eyes, sniffling.

"What's he expect me to do?" she demanded. Admittedly, running away from him wasn't going to solve the problem either, but he'd probably teleported back to Aesir by now.

As she'd expected, it began raining. A rolling wall of water tore through the canopy, soaking everything below almost instantly. Folding her ears down, Astra continued slogging forward. It wasn't like she had access to her Inventory to pull out a poncho or something, so she dealt with it.

The path she followed came close to the stream again, but this time, the waters had gotten considerably rougher. She kept a healthy distance from the bank, but kept sight of it, since she couldn't smell or hear it over the sound of the rain.

Where am I even going? she wondered. *What was the point?*

Except if there was a Soul Stone in the Southlands, then she could attune to it and never show her face in the north again. That would prevent Xander from being in danger from other Porters wanting to make a Pact with her.

She pushed her hair back from her face, knowing she was still crying.

"Yeah, I joined something I thought was a game. It turned out not to be. How was I supposed to know? It wasn't like Xan could tell me."

Shuffling from the bushes made her stop. Looking over, she found a Razor Boar. Examining it revealed that not only was it targeting her, but it had a much higher level.

Astra turned and went in the only direction she had available. Xander's Shelter had worn off a while ago. She needed to go somewhere the Boar couldn't easily get to. Clambering up onto a fallen log, she scooted out over the rapidly flooding stream and yelped when the Boar struck the base of the log. A sickening crack told her she'd made the wrong choice, just before she hit the water.

Struggling to the surface, she gasped for air once, then took the broken log to the face and was pushed under. It caught a buckle on her armor, dragging her beneath it as the rushing water pushed them both downstream.

Astra fought with the buckle, trying to get it undone, trying to break the branch she was caught on. A sudden drop brought her face out of the water. She let her breath out, intending to catch a fresh gulp of air. The rocks at the bottom of the fall knocked the wind out of her.

The rushing water rolled the log over again, scraping her face against the bottom.

In a panic, she flailed, trying to get to the surface. Water rushed into her throat.

She coughed; sucked in more.

Vomited, sucked in more.

* * *

Night had fallen and Astra was still moving farther away, heading in a generally southward direction. Xander only paused long enough to pull out something he could eat on the run and kept going.

The rain continued, although it had gotten less torrential as the sun went down.

When darkness descended fully, Xander stopped again. It had been a while since he'd run like this, but he didn't feel too exhausted. Looking through Astra's Inventory again, he found a lamp. Tying it to his belt, he started moving again, the enchanted light bouncing and throwing strange shadows on the ground. It almost made the trek more dangerous. It was hard to tell how deep each shadow was until he stepped in it and nearly twisted his ankle.

Forced to slow, Xander could feel the distance to Astra's corpse growing. How long would she wait for him before returning to Aesir's Soul Stone? It had already been hours, but now she was several miles away and showed no signs of stopping.

What happened to her?

Around midnight, he tripped over a branch he could barely see in the dark and hit the mud, leg screaming in pain. Xander lay there a moment, knowing he'd broken it, but having also hit his head on something and seeing stars. He couldn't continue jogging. His stamina had run out.

Once he caught his breath, he cast Cure to fix the physical damage and checked his Directional Sense to find that Astra had finally stopped. But she was thirty miles away now.

"I can travel that distance on flat land pretty fast," he muttered, still on his hands and knees in the mud. "But the terrain is not ideal." It would take him at least another day to reach her. She hadn't sent herself back to Aesir yet, which was reassuring.

However, he knew firsthand what being dead for hours felt like.

"Just... stay there, Astra," he sighed and got to his feet to start walking again, trying to be careful of the slick rocks and branches. The terrain had become quite steep, leading down as he followed the stream. Maybe she'd fallen in? That was the only explanation he could come to that made any sense. But surely, she knew how to swim? He'd seen her swim before.

When dawn broke, the sky was still overcast and drizzling.

Staggering to a stop, Xander dropped to his knees in the mud. He'd barely traveled seven miles in the dark, but it had been rough. His path hadn't been straight down. Downed trees blocked his path, boulders, the stream itself had flooded sections and he had to go around.

Astra still waited.

He pulled out her Menu and searched through her Inventory for something to eat, deciding to take something hearty and eat sitting down. Xander pulled his sodden hair out of his face and tried not to feel guilty. Astra had never left him dead for more than two or three hours. That had only been because they were in a battle zone, and she couldn't afford to take the time from protecting herself. She'd never left him behind.

"I've been worse to her than she ever was to me," he muttered, failing in warding off the sinking feeling in his chest. At this point, he wouldn't have blamed her if she went ahead and sent herself back to Aesir.

A momentary death consisted of intense pain, then darkness with residual pain upon revival. Longer times came with the feeling of being chewed apart, piece by piece, losing yourself to that darkness. Did it feel the same to Immortals, though? Xander suspected the suffering he and others endured was the soul itself losing purchase on the body. He had come across corpses several days old before and could see white sparks floating off them. He could tell how old they were by the glow and whether it was possible to bring them back. The sparks staved off animals and maggots from settling in, but only for up to five days. By then, the soul was completely gone, and Resurrect would have no effect.

Finishing his meal, Xander staggered to his feet and started walking again.

He would make better time today. He was determined to.

A break in the trees allowed him a view of the terrain ahead. The stream he had been following did indeed empty into a massive lake at the bottom of the slope. However, the trek down was going to continue to be grueling.

Not seeing an easy way down from the boulder he stood on, Xander turned back the way he came and started trying to find a new path. The sidetrack added another mile to his journey before he could zag back on course.

Further ill luck found him when he stumbled into a pack of Rush Thorns. The mobile plants with thorny vines were highly aggressive towards other creatures and immediately attacked as he pushed through the foliage.

"[Shelter]," he cast after the first strike hit him. He'd not taken much damage, all things considered, but he didn't think they were going to leave him alone unless he gave them something else to worry about.

"[Raise Undead]," he cast, calling the fifty meat Golems from the earth. "Attack," he ordered his army.

The Rush Thorns turned to take on the creatures that were actively attacking them. Xander pushed through the pack and left them behind.

He felt his Undead collapse one by one and knew that they'd not done much damage to the monsters. His summons had only made one kill out of the twenty monsters there. Thankfully Rush Thorns weren't fast, and they did not come after him. They weren't the only monsters he encountered along the way. He ignored those he could and killed the ones he couldn't ignore. He ended up with three Razor Boar carcasses and a Treefoil in his inventory before he hit the rocky beach of the lake in the late afternoon.

Staring out at the water, he could feel that Astra was some distance still, but he didn't see her.

Xander followed the shore as far as he could to get closer. Once he was within five hundred feet, he waded into the water and started swimming towards the log flow that cluttered near the end of the stream he'd been following all night.

Exhausted, he threw an arm over the first log he got to for a moment of rest. Still, there was no indication of where Astra's corpse was. Pulling himself onto the log he clung to, he straddled it for a slightly better viewpoint.

In the distance, he spotted a spark of light off something tall and shiny on the shoreline, but the sun dipped below the mountains surrounding the lake, leaving the whole area in gloom.

"Where are you...?" Xander muttered. He needed to lay eyes on her to cast. But if she was underwater and he did that, she ran the risk of dying again.

Scooting along the log, he climbed onto the next entangled one.

The water rippled and thrashed to his right.

Activating the lantern, Xander lifted it to look, finding what looked like a white tail floating on the surface.

Diving into the water again, he swam over, groping in the dark water until he found the base of that tail. Grasping her hips, he pulled, but doing so tugged the log next to her.

Blindly groping, he followed her back. Xander ducked under the water and finally found the problem. A strap on her arm guard had gotten tangled on a branch. He popped to the surface for a breath, then dove back down. The strap was hopelessly twisted up, holding Astra's neck close to the broken log. Pulling his knife, Xander started sawing at the leather.

Unfortunately, her armor was too high-quality to simply cut through.

Coming up for air again, Xander gripped the log as he tried to think of how to handle this. Splashing around in the lake in the dark would get him into trouble soon enough. He could sense monsters lurking in the depths.

Ducking back under, he tried tackling the branch she was attached to, only to end up hurting himself more than he damaged it.

Again, he needed to breathe.

"No help for it," Xander said and reached for Astra's Menu. Treading water and dealing with the menu at the same time wasn't easy, but he found her equipment information and unequipped her shoulder guards and chest armor, unsure which one exactly had gotten tangled.

Something passed beneath him.

Astra's body was on the move again, heading deeper.

Xander shoved the Scroll into his pocket, but it slipped from his hand before it was secure.

Diving, he swam as hard as he could after the corpse thief.

The lake monster was intercepted by something larger. Xander was only aware of it on an instinctual level. But luckily, the corpse thief released Astra's body. With just enough time to grab her around the waist, Xander swam for the surface, dragging her with him, then struggled towards shore before the two monsters figured out who would be dining on whom this evening.

Dragging them both up the rocky shore, Xander collapsed to his knees to catch his breath. Lifting the lamp, he looked at her. She had abrasions across her face, and a gash on her forehead. Pale from blood loss, her skin was puffy from prolonged submersion. The worrying part was the sparks of life surrounding her were nearly gone.

"[Resurrect]," he cast. Her health returned immediately. "[Cure]," he added, bringing her up to full, clearing out whatever water remained in her lungs instantly.

She breathed, opened her eyes, and stared at him with no recognition.

Xander had seen that look before in others he'd brought back just barely in time. It would take a while for her to recover mentally. Gathering her against his chest, he staggered to his feet again and walked towards the ruins he could barely make out a short distance from the shore. Finding the remains of a stone building, he entered and set her down.

Pulling the rugs and blankets from his Inventory, he stripped his own equipment and wrapped them both together. It was going to be a cold night and he doubted he'd be able to find any dry firewood after the rains. Better to just share body heat.

Exhausted, he closed his eyes, holding Astra tight as she started to shiver.

The darkness haunted her, although this darkness was warm and broken by gentle breathing beside her.

It encouraged rest, which she allowed herself to fall into for a time until there was a sliver of light in the darkness. Still, the heartbeat beside her was calm, the cocoon of warmth reassuring, but Astra could hear birds and the sound of water on rocks.

I drowned, she realized. *Someone brought me back... Xander came and got me.* She recognized his scent. Moving against him slightly, she realized that neither of them was fully dressed.

What happened?

The rhythm of his heartbeat changed slightly. Lifting the blankets, Xander let some light into their cocoon.

Astra tipped her head to look up at him. His hair was a tangled mess. He had streaks of mud in it and across his face. He seemed to approve of what he saw and lowered his arm, tucking the blankets back around them.

"What're you doing?" she asked.

"Getting some more sleep," Xander said. "I chased your corpse for a full day and a half."

Her ears folded down. She'd been dead for that long?

Astra remembered the first few hours. The option to respawn had been there. She considered doing it... But if Xander had gone back to Aesir, then she'd just be dropping herself back into his business again. So, she'd left it. What did it matter anyway? As time had passed... she'd felt that option slipping further and further from her grasp. By the time she'd decided that maybe she should just respawn, the option was no longer there at all.

Then the cold had settled in. The freezing grip of death

chipped away at the edges of her consciousness.

"Who asked you to?" Astra whispered. "You could've just gone back to your life and left me."

Xander sighed.

Astra struggled to free herself from the blankets and sat up, finding that she wore nothing but her leather pants and undershirt. Folding her arms over her chest, she glared at him.

Sitting up, Xander tiredly tucked the blankets around his waist. He'd stripped down to his pants, leaving his pale chest bare. He scrubbed his hand against his cheek, rubbing some of the dried mud off.

She looked away. Despite being a Healer Class, he still had quite a bit of muscle on his skinny frame. It was distracting to look at.

"We need to discuss what happened," he said finally.

"There's nothing to say," Astra insisted, although she wasn't sure about which 'what happened' he meant.

"I took my anger out on you," Xander said. "You weren't aware of the damage you were causing. You couldn't have known. I apologize."

Pulling her knees to her chest, Astra turned her back to him. "It isn't like you don't have a right to be mad," she admitted.

"Be that as it may, I do not have the right to be angry on the part of others. Especially those who are long dead. It has been five hundred years since the Immortals left. We do not have confirmation that you are alone in returning, but regardless... You were not one of the worst offenders. Given the circumstances, you treated me well."

"You were still a slave, essentially," Astra muttered

into her knees. "Treating you better than I could've doesn't make it right."

"You had no way of knowing I was sentient," Xander said. "I forgive you."

Astra didn't want to continue the conversation. It didn't matter if he forgave her. She didn't forgive herself. "I'll send you back to Aesir," she said instead.

"I lost the Menu."

She could swear her heart stopped.

Turning to look at him, she found him in the process of equipping his armor. He dropped her leather chest armor and shoulder guards beside her.

"You were tangled with a log. When I got you loose, a lake monster stole your body and I had to take chase again. I lost the Menu in the lake," Xander said.

Astra couldn't find words. Her mouth opened and closed a few times before she settled on just silence and put her chin on her knees.

"Do you happen to know how to cook without Crafting?" Xander asked. "I have Razor Boar meat in my inventory."

"Yeah, but it won't be very good," she said.

"Better than nothing," Xander said and stood, heading out into the sunlight, his filthy hair glittering like stars.

But what was the point? Her Menu was gone and that had been her hope of being able to log out. So now she was just stuck, waiting for her body to die and take her with it? The uncertainty was maddening, and she could not get her hands to close correctly over the buckles for her armor.

Disgusted with herself, she stood, tumbled to the

ground, and ended up crawling out of the ruined building to the beach. Where she was going, she had no idea. Throwing rocks at the water seemed like a nice idea, but she could barely get her hands around them. They kept slipping from her weak fingers.

* * *

He could still sense the grip death had on her. Her mind had returned, but her spirit was still not recovered.

Xander couldn't help the guilt as he glanced out at the lake every time he picked up a piece of driftwood. If he'd not let her just charge off like that... if he could find her Menu... On the other hand, it was a hint that Immortals could die permanently if they were prevented from going to a Soul Stone. He wasn't sure how he felt about that knowledge.

Returning to Astra, he found her picking through the rocks on the beach, a distant look in her eyes. She'd not put her armor back on. The rocks fell from her fingers frequently, as if she didn't have full control of her hands, she didn't even seem to know what she was doing. She was not okay.

Dropping the load of branches, he started setting up a campfire but wasn't looking forward to what he would have to do to light it. He considered trying to pull some threads and fur off the blankets and rugs. Considering their quality, though, he doubted he'd be able to, much the way he hadn't been able to cut Astra's armor the night before.

She looked up at him for a moment, then back down at her rocks. "I can't seem to move very well," she said.

"Side effect of being close to permanent death," Xander said.

"Oh… so, I can die if I don't respawn in time."

"Apparently." He glanced at her. "Usually, it takes longer to reach that point."

"Maybe I didn't want to live," she said.

Xander set down the stick he held. "Why would you give up like that?"

She didn't look at him, didn't speak.

"One heated discussion and you decide that dying is your best option?" Xander asked. Her ears twitched. Her hair was hopelessly matted.

"Wouldn't it be better that way? One less Immortal to worry about."

"No."

"Then I'm to spend the rest of my immortality atoning for my sins," Astra said dully.

Putting his hand to his eyes, Xander sighed. He'd never been very good with people's emotions. This situation was incredibly uncomfortable. He honestly didn't know what to do.

"Astra Diane—"

"Jessica," she said.

"What?"

"That's my real name. The one my mother gave me."

Xander hesitated a moment, then asked, "Do you wish to return to your world?"

"What's the point of that?" she asked. "I've got nothing there either."

Recalling what she'd said of her past, Xander lowered his hand to his lap. While he'd spent the last five hundred years using the Skills she'd given him to improve his lot in life, she didn't carry any of that over to her daily life. She was only powerful here in Ashguard, and even then, compared to any of the Cursed Ones, she would be very little challenge. She'd come to Ashguard as a relief from her miserable life only to find herself stuck and despised by her only companion.

"I am sorry," Xander said. "Jessica. I have been nothing but unkind to you."

"Nah," she said, still looking at her pile of rocks. "I really should be used to it by now." The smile she gave was bitter.

Left with no way to make it better, Xander turned back to trying to make a fire.

* * *

It had taken hours, but Xander got the fire going. At least by that time, she could wrap her hands around things and hold them. However, she couldn't hold the knife with any sort of accuracy and Xander had been forced to hack up the Boar meat. The best she could manage was huge hunks of meat speared on sticks and set over the fire. And Xander now had a mutilated carcass that probably could've been better utilized in his Inventory. Fat dripped off the meat, sizzling on the rocks below.

Xander had brought the blankets and rugs over, folded up so they had somewhere soft to sit, but Astra ignored it in favor of sitting on the rocks. She knew she was just wallowing and punishing herself, but she honestly didn't feel like she deserved better. Maybe her whole life on

Earth had been as bad as it was because she deserved to be punished? The familiar ache in her heart brought tears to her eyes, but she didn't want to cry in front of Xander. She didn't want his pity.

Now without her Menu, she was nearly useless. Sure, she could use her combat Skills, but her crafting Skills were out of reach. She needed her Menu to access recipes.

"Keep the fire going," Xander said and stood.

She gazed after him as he headed towards the water's edge and started slogging in, swimming towards the drift of logs some five or six hundred feet away. What was he doing?

Astra looked towards the fire. It was steady and did not need any tending. The Boar meat was burning on one side. She turned them, then went back to stacking rocks. Her motor control was getting better. Probably by evening, she would be moving normally. She didn't care. Why hadn't he left her? He had every right to be angry. Now she knew he was feeling sorry for her and that was the last thing she wanted.

I could get up and walk off, she considered. *But he would be able to track her down. I have to make him leave me then.*

Taking a breath, she let it out, finding a spark of fire. She looked out at the water. What was he even doing? That water didn't look pleasant to swim in.

Something rippled in the water as he got to the log flow and threw an arm over one of the logs to take a rest. He was pulled under from below.

Astra stood and went to the edge of the water but knew that she wouldn't be able to do anything. His HP was still full. He bobbed back up some distance from where he'd gone under, wiped his hair out of his face, then dove.

Was he taking revenge on the lake monsters that had tried to eat her?

She shook her head and decided to leave him to it. Turning to go back to the fire, she yelped as she found someone crouching beside it, eating one of the sticks of meat.

Astra stayed still. The kid, a Lycanth child with mostly Human features, laid his ears back, eyes growing wide. He stuck the stick of meat in his mouth and darted off down the beach.

If there was a child here... there had to be more people.

She followed at a slower jog, keeping the boy in view, but not closing the distance.

The child panicked, running along the beach to where the mountains practically dipped into the lake. The forest covered the side of the mountain, but as she got closer, Astra could tell there were structures between the trees. For that matter, to her left were the remains of a sizeable city. She'd been too in her feelings to notice earlier. Now, she perked her ears. She could hear people and smelled cooking fires. There was a village here.

The familiar tinkling of bells on the wind tickled her senses.

There was a Soul Stone here!

Leaving off chasing the boy, Astra changed her path towards the mountain and entered the trees.

People, a mix of Lycanth, Felis, and Human, stopped to stare at her as she passed them. The people wore rustic clothes of furs and leather, their buildings were stone with wooden shingle roofs and roads were mostly mud with the occasional cobblestone. Astra followed the most used route to the central square where a Soul Stone of a different design than those in Aesir, Vanaheim, and Nifelheim stood. Reaching out towards it, she connected and attuned, changing her respawn point.

* * *

Slogging out of the water, his mission unsuccessful, Xander wiped his wet hair from his face and looked towards the unattended fire.

It hadn't gone out, but Astra was not there.

He sighed. Had she run off again? His Directional Sense told him she wasn't that far away and in good health still. She was a little to the south, just around the shore of the lake, towards the mountains. Approaching the fire, he found one stick of meat left. It was charred.

Tossing some more wood onto the fire to keep it going, he started after Astra. Did she really think she could just hide from him or something?

He found her sitting on a log on the beach, whittling a stick with his knife, which he had left with her so she could cut meat. Xander stopped beside her, hands on his hips as he looked down at her. "I asked you to tend the fire."

"You didn't ask. You told," Astra said and looked up at him. Standing, she held the knife out, hilt first. "Here's your knife back. You can go back to Aesir now."

He made no move to take the knife.

"There's a Soul Stone here," Astra said. "If I die, I'll

respawn here," she said. "You won't have to see me ever again."

"That won't stop the others from coming after me," Xander said. "I will stay with you a while longer." He stared down at her. She still had Death's touch in her eyes. He did decide to take the knife from her. He was kind of glad he hadn't been able to find her Menu. With it, she could forcibly send him back to Aesir. "So, there is a Soul Stone here," he said.

"And a village," Astra said, gesturing up the slope.

He turned to look, finding what looked like village hunters crouched among the trees, watching.

"Did you not introduce yourself?" Xander asked.

"I attuned to their Soul Stone and came out to the beach to show them I meant their village no harm." Astra turned away, looking out across the lake. "Did you have fun with the monsters out there?"

Deciding that acting aggressively towards her, no matter how irritated she was making him, would do little good, Xander sheathed the knife and put it into his Inventory. "You could have gone back to our camp," he said.

"I didn't want to."

"You're being incredibly stubborn," Xander said.

Astra looked up at him with a toothy grin. "Glad you noticed. Go home, Xander."

"I will not," he said. "Respect should go both ways. If I am not allowed to order you to tend the fire, you may not order me to leave."

Her tail flicked in irritation.

Xander placed his hand on her shoulder. "Jessica," he

said gently, "you are not well. I cannot leave you."

She shrugged his hand off. "I'm fine!" She moved away. "I've got all my fingers and toes. I'm breathing."

"You got too close to death, and it still calls you," Xander stated bluntly.

"What does that even matter to you?" she demanded, stepping back and facing him, her ears flat. "You don't want Immortals around anyway."

Refusing to raise his voice in return, Xander kept silent.

Her tail lashed in anger as she glared up at him. "Ugh!" She turned away, folding her arms, everything about her posture angry.

Xander left her to that and instead headed up the rocky beach towards the waiting hunters. "Greetings," he said. He suspected that the ones he could see were a fraction of the ones he couldn't. "I am Xander, my companion is Astra."

Chapter 4

Astra followed Xander as they were led back into the village. She'd tried to be respectful of the people who lived there when she'd visited the first time by attuning to the Soul Stone and getting back out without looking at anyone or their stuff. She had known they were keeping an eye on her at the beach. She had also suspected that going back to Xander's fire would have raised suspicions. Astra honestly didn't know how first contact with lost tribes was supposed to go.

Xander seemed to be handling it well, though. He had calmly talked his way into getting to see their elder, and now they were on their way back to the central square.

An old Lycanth woman with mostly wolf features stood leaning on her staff, her greying fur covering her eyes. "It has been a long time since we have seen outsiders," the old woman said. "I am Ruth."

Tail flicking in curiosity, Astra almost asked her question but recalled that Xander was probably better at speaking to these people.

"We thank you for withholding judgment," Xander said. "I am Xander, this is Astra Diane."

"Your companion can speak to the Soul Stone," the old woman said. "We cannot attack those chosen by the gods."

Astra's ears folded down. "So, you've seen people who cannot die before?" breaking her silence.

"In legends very old," the ancient Lycanth woman

said. "Stories passed down from when we first settled here."

"Five hundred years ago," Xander said.

The Lycanth laughed. "Far older, boy," she said. "Come. Follow me." She turned and started shuffling towards the mountain. "Ashguard is far older than anyone knows, ruins of long dead civilizations are littered across the lands and even the seas. The Great Cycle has wiped out every one of them before long, despite the gods protecting us with their very bodies. Since the disasters that befell our world came from outside this dimension, the gods chose to look outside our dimension for an answer... and found Nox."

As she spoke, they reached a doorway built directly into the mountain. Entering when attendants opened the doors, Ruth gestured with her walking staff at the plaques of writing on every wall.

Astra's ears flicked down, recognizing the plaques as crystal, much like that of the Soul Stones, but she could not read what they said.

Xander was practically vibrating and jogged forward to turn and look up at the plaques mounted above the door. "This is—the Holy Writ!" he whispered in awe. "But it is complete! The ones in Aesir, Vanaheim, and Nifelheim are partial and broken!"

She couldn't help but smile at his enthusiasm. It was... rather cute. On multiple occasions, she'd been chastised by other Players for taking an Elf as her Porter. Elves naturally had higher dexterity, stamina, and hearing, making them better suited to Warrior roles. She'd been told that she'd deprived a Player of a meat shield. Seeing him now, Astra decided, *No. He likes being a scholar.*

"When Vard was overrun by demons and monsters from the Convergence, we retreated here. Geist, our patron god, protected the sanctuary, but he could not withstand the onslaught and died. We were saved but cut off from the rest of the world."

Xander shook his head in disbelief. "This is Vard? The Convergence that destroyed Vard was nearly two thousand years ago. How have you remained unfound for so long?"

"The monsters roaming the mountains and forests are more powerful than we can defeat by ourselves. Our numbers remain small due to that," the Lycanth woman explained. She walked further into the large, empty, stone room; her cane clacking echoes on the floor. "I believe even you heroes had trouble reaching us."

Astra flicked her ears down in shame. "Wouldn't have been that hard if I wasn't acting stupid," she admitted.

"I had a hand in that," Xander reminded.

She shot him a look, then decided to ignore him.

"It is fortunate that we have been rediscovered now," Ruth said. "A Convergence is coming."

"A—what?" Astra asked and turned to look at the woman. "What's a Convergence?"

Xander's gaze remained fixed on the plaques, mouth moving slightly as he read them. "She's right," he said and pointed. "The Star of Calamity has risen in the southern skies and the five Lights of the Damned..." He withdrew his finger and looked worried.

"Ashguard is just another world on the belt of stars," Ruth said. "Another world, brushes against ours every so often, opening portals all over the lands, allowing powerful monsters through. Those that are not killed make Ashguard their home."

Xander tore himself away from the plaques to look at Astra and Ruth. "We haven't much time and we are sorely unprepared... although there are a little over a hundred Cursed Ones remaining many may not wish to join the fight."

"Want to join?" Astra asked, hands going to her hips. "By the sounds of it, the fight's going to come to them. They either fight or die." Her ears perked, then folded again. "I don't have any Weapon Skills," she said.

"What Skills do you have?" the old woman asked.

"Healer Class mostly. A bunch of crafting... but I don't have my Menu, so I can't even make Scrolls."

"Menu?"

"Yeah... it's what I use to interact with the System," Astra said.

"Perhaps another can be made?" the Lycanth asked.

Astra shrugged. "I don't know. I've never heard of anyone losing their Menu before..."

"In the meantime," Xander said, "Are there Skill Masters here?"

"Many. We did our best to perfect the Skills we had and preserve the knowledge," Ruth said.

Astra stared at Xander, ears down. "What are you doing?"

"We came out here to level you up," Xander said as he stood over her. "There are Skills here that you do not have and plenty of monsters upon which to practice them. I will continue to support you."

"But I can't make Scrolls..." Astra objected. Xander

turned her shoulders and guided her out of the building.

"We will worry about that later. Perhaps there is a way to make a new Menu in one of the other cities. Or perhaps we will find yours in the lake. Either way, you cannot make a Scroll for a Skill you haven't leveled up."

Feeling cornered, Astra had little choice but to go where he pushed her, following the Lycanth elder.

* * *

Ruth led them up the road a short distance to another building. The houses in Vard were old but obviously rebuilt from the rubble of structures closer to the shore. They consisted of stone block foundations overlayed with wooden decking and a narrow porch along the front. The windows were merely shuttered holes in walls. The destination Ruth had in mind was another such house with a flat cobblestone yard in front. Three boys were practicing archery on targets set against the flat, windowless side of the building. One girl was working with a sword on a wooden dummy on the opposite side.

Astra pointed at one of the boys. "That's the kid that stole your lunch," she said to Xander.

"Then that was yours you left to burn?" Xander asked.

She shrugged at him. "I wasn't going to eat either one of them," she admitted. "I have standards."

Admittedly so did he.

They passed through the courtyard; the Lycanth boy who had been pointed out looking at them nervously with his ears pinned down.

The old Human that sat on the porch watching the

children lifted a brow as they approached. "Our mysterious visitors come to speak to me?" he asked.

The Lycanth elder smiled, her dulled teeth showing. "This one is an Immortal, come to receive your teaching." She gestured at Astra.

With spryness that belied his age, the man jumped to his feet. "You jest! She looks like one of us!"

Astra's tail flicked briefly. Xander wasn't quite sure what her hesitation was for, so he spoke. "It is true, sir."

"Come! Let me give you my Scroll!" the man hurried into the building. The children had given up pretending to do their practice and instead hurried to watch as Astra followed the man inside.

Xander chose to give Ruth a hand climbing the steps and arrived in time to see the Human man offer the ancient Scroll to Astra.

Bowing as she took it, Astra said, "Thank you for your knowledge."

"I'm just happy to have it go to someone that can use its full potential."

Unrolling the Scroll, it flashed, disappearing in her hands. For a moment, Astra stared at the air, gaze darting around as she read. "Huh," she mused.

"I have several more from my forefathers," the man said excitedly and started pulling them out of a drawer. The drawer was practically packed.

Astra's ears folded back. "I don't know if I've got time to level all of these..." she said in a small voice.

"Take them," Xander said. "You only need to get them to fifty before you can hand out copies."

"Right..." she mumbled and opened another Scroll. It

flashed and disappeared.

By the time she got through them all, Astra looked exhausted.

"Is the Immortal here?" a woman called from the door.

"Yes, yes, she is right here," the weapons master said excitedly. "Come in, Glen!"

The woman that entered was likely in her mid-forties, a mostly Human-looking Felis with tabby markings on her skin. Over her shoulder, she had a satchel full to the brim with Scrolls. Glen's eyes strayed to Xander with the slightest of smiles.

Astra's ears were flat to her skull, but she took the Scrolls she was handed. That was the first of five more Skill Masters that came to Astra with their offerings.

Ruth pulled Xander's arm gently, drawing him away while Astra was busy.

"You are her apprentice, correct?" the old Lycanth asked.

"Ah... yes." Xander decided to just go with that since the situation was complicated.

"She seems unwell."

"The story is complicated," Xander said. "I will take care of her."

Ruth nodded but didn't look entirely convinced. "You seem very mature for someone your age."

Laughing softly, Xander shook his head. "I am over five hundred."

Her ears perked from their constant droop, brows raising enough to lift the hair out of her eyes. "How is such a thing possible? Our oldest Elf was two hundred and thirty. You look barely older than a child."

"A byproduct of being an Immortal's apprentice," Xander said.

"You said 'Cursed Ones' before," Ruth prodded.

"It is... a long and less than pleasant story." Xander really didn't want to taint these people against Astra, but this woman was not going to take no for an answer. "There were immortals five hundred years ago. They took apprentices, passed on the Skills they had, then left again. However, those who had been bound to them remained unageing. Our Skills remain unlocked. However, any Skills we pass along are locked at fifty."

Ruth straightened her curved spine to look up at him. "But the Soul Binding can only be performed once. How have you come to serve Lady Astra?"

"She was the one I apprenticed to five hundred years ago. She returned. Although I know not of any other Immortals," Xander said.

"Ah. The ways of Immortals are not for us to know," Ruth said.

Xander nodded, letting it go at that.

"You mentioned one of her Holy Items was lost in the lake? I'm afraid you'll not recover it. The monsters within are too dangerous for us to attempt to help."

"I'll send Undead," Astra said. She looked a little dazed. "I still have access to my combat Skills."

"Ah," Xander said. "They can scour the bottom of the lake while you work on other things. First, you must eat."

On cue, her stomach growled.

* * *

121

Over fifty new Skills later and Astra felt exhausted as if someone had written on her already tired soul with needles. The first fifteen had been melee and ranged weapons. These were such in-depth Skills that they had their own names rather than simply being Piercing Mastery, Bashing Mastery, and such. The lance Skill was called Dragoon. The bare fist martial arts were Monk. She already had Sword and Shield as payment from another Player but she'd never gotten any Sword Skill or Shield Skill to make use of it. It appeared, if a Player Scroll worked with a Skill she got from a Skill Master, the Player Skill Scroll would unlock fully. Her new talents Blademaster and Bulwark had unlocked Sword and Shield, allowing her to level it beyond one hundred.

The people of Vard had been so excited to finally have people from outside find them that they'd built a bonfire in the Soul Stone Plaza and brought out chairs and tables for a feast. Xander, having nothing else to use the meat on, had donated the Razor Boars he had in his inventory and the villagers had joined with more food.

Astra stared blankly at the fire, hands dangling between her thighs. Evening had fallen. She couldn't get her eyes to focus.

A familiar blanket settled around her shoulders. She looked up at Xander as he sat beside her on the ground.

"We need to speak of what happened," Xander said.

"We already did, and it doesn't matter," Astra said.

"It does. There is more at stake than my wounded feelings. Regardless of how you came to this world, your presence is desperately needed."

"So, you're willing to put aside everything the Players

did and use me because the world is in danger," Astra interpreted. She shifted, pulling the blanket closer and over her head, blocking out the sight of him. "Never mind the fact that my real body is just lying there in my apartment, dying," she added. "I could just fizzle away at any moment for all I know."

"Astra—" he started, then leaned to look at her face, his hair a sparkling curtain between her and the fire. "Jessica," he amended.

"Get out of my face," she muttered. "I didn't say I wasn't going to do what I can."

He leaned out of her field of view, but suddenly swept her up in his arms and stood.

Yelping, she clutched his shoulder. "Where are you taking me?"

"To bed. You need rest."

"I don't want to." She kept her voice low, aware that others were within hearing. "Please... Stop..." she whispered, starting to tremble.

They entered a darkened house and Xander sat her on a soft bed. Kneeling at her feet, he gazed up at her face, his eyes searching her. She could only tell his features because he was so pale that what little light there was reflected off his skin.

"I will not leave you alone," Xander said. "It is my fault you were dead for so long. It is my fault that you nearly lost the will to live. I will take responsibility and stay by your side, Jessica. You will not be alone this night or any other until you feel ready for such."

Flushing, she looked away. Was he... saying what she thought he was? Did he like her? Surely not. *No... it... no.*

Pushing him away gently, she fell onto her side and rolled over in the bed, putting her back to him.

The bed moved as he laid down behind her, the blanket tucked tightly around her along with his arms. "Sleep now. Tomorrow will be long." She felt him pet her hair down, gently rubbing her ear and the space just in front of it.

Astra had done that to cats before, but to have it done to her...

Her eyes fell shut in pleasure. She couldn't resist the pull of sleep.

* * *

Xander was vaguely aware that Astra had woken several times in the night but had settled back down after shifting position on the bed. At a point late in the evening, he'd been awoken by her sniffles. Obviously, she'd been trying not to wake him as she cried.

Xander had chosen to pretend to sleep. Admittedly, she was in a tough situation. Was she going to die along with her body? It had only been a few days in Ashguard, but she had said that time flowed differently between the realms.

Now that he knew the desperate situation Ashguard was in, they couldn't afford to lose her. He didn't know how long they had before the Convergence. He didn't know how long Astra had before her body died. He didn't know if she would disappear from Ashguard if her body did die. There were too many unknowns, and he didn't like it. One thing he could prevent, however, was Astra seeking death on her own.

She had been far too close to death, and he had seen many succumb to the darkness in the days after a late Resurrection. So, he had laid down with her. He hadn't meant to touch her so intimately. Xander had been trying to get her gross, lake water-crusty hair out of his mouth, but when he'd pet her ear, the reaction was immediate. She was instantly asleep. Unfortunately for him, there was no getting comfortable in that bed. It had not been made for someone of his height and it wasn't very wide, which meant that he'd been curled against Astra's back the entire night.

He cracked his eye open, finding morning light seeping between the slats of the shutters on the window. He unexpectedly had the bed to himself.

Sitting up, he glanced towards their health bars at the top left of his vision and was relieved to find that she was at full health. Consulting his Direction Sense, he felt that she wasn't far away, simply up the street.

Tossing the blanket off, he ran his hands through his disgusting hair, equipped his armor, and opened the door to a glorious woodland morning.

Following the road up the slope, he came to the communal kitchen that had prepared their feast the night before. Here, he found Astra, ears up and tail swaying with interest as she helped in the kitchen, filling flat discs of dough with leftovers from the previous night. Her hair was clean, dried into loose waves around her face. She wore a loose shirt and pants of local fashion.

Looking up from her work, she left off her dough and went to a plate, picking a few steamed buns off the top to hand to him. "There's a bathhouse just down there," she said, pointing.

Xander nodded, taking the steamed buns and heading off to find said location. Biting into one, he stopped in surprise and actually [Examined] the item he held.

[Steamed Bun, Level 334, Boost to Stamina Duration 5 hours: Crafter Astra Diane]

Apparently, she still had access to her crafting Skills without her Menu. That was good news—and probably why she was in such a good mood. Finding the bathhouse, Xander stepped in, having to duck through the doorway as usual. The problem was that he didn't have any clothes to wear except his disgusting armor, he realized and was about to turn around to go back when the Felis Mage Skill Master burst in.

"Oh!" she gasped. She was tawny brown with mostly Human features but tabby markings on her skin. "Here." She held out a bundle of cloth. "Astra said you didn't have anything else to wear."

"She is correct," Xander said and took the bundle. "Thank you." Glen, he recalled finally. Her name was Glen.

The smile the woman gave him was shy. He knew it meant that she found him attractive and was vaguely hoping something might happen between them. Instead, he took a bite of the steamed bun and tucked the clothes under his arm, heading further into the bathhouse. The Felis woman's ears flicked down in disappointment, but she left him alone. Finishing his breakfast, Xander stripped his leathers and began by washing his hair.

* * *

She knew she was probably misinterpreting, Astra couldn't help but feel something tight in her chest as she'd looked down at Xander's sleeping face that morning. He had ended up on his back with her curled beneath his arm, head on his chest. The man slept so quietly she'd resorted to putting her ear near his nose. He snorted and twitched as her hair tickled him. Even wearing several days' filth, he was stunning to look at.

Sitting back, Astra brushed her hand over her ear and hair, remembering how he'd pet her. She didn't know what to make of him... Did he have feelings for her, or was it strictly business? The way he acted most of the day versus how he had been sleeping with her for the last two nights were just so different.

Mentally doing math, Astra guessed that it had been somewhere around two to three days on Earth. She didn't feel any different. Would the death of her body sneak up on her? What would it feel like? She wasn't going to get anything leveled in time to hand it on to others, and with her Menu gone, she couldn't make Scrolls of the ones she already had leveled up enough. Why had they all jumped on board this plan?

Unable to come to any kind of conclusion, she decided that maybe she should just keep herself busy until the end.

Stepping out the door, she found a redheaded Felis standing at the foot of the stairs, holding a bundle of clothes.

"Hi! I'm Rita," the woman said. "Yesterday looked pretty tough for you, they didn't even let you get cleaned up."

Astra pushed her chin-length white hair out of her face

and cringed when she hit a tangle.

"Come with me. We'll get you washed up," Rita said and stepped up one stair to grab Astra's wrist, pulling her down the street while she continued talking. "Welcome to Vard. We're what's left of a bigger city, or so Ruth has said. The rest of the city is under the lake."

Looking in that direction, Astra could see the murky blue water between the trees and houses.

"We have a lot of community buildings here. I don't know what it's like in other cities, but we really rely on each other to survive. I'm one of the five cooks. We rotate out morning and night."

They arrived at another building and Rita pulled Astra's arm, bringing her up the two steps to the porch and then into the building. "This is our bathhouse." The room they entered was one big space with multiple spigots on the walls and benches beneath them. "We wash in here and then the next room is a hot bath, but we don't heat that up until closer to the evenings. The hunters usually come in with sore muscles and bruises and soak then."

Before Astra could do anything, Rita was stripping her clothes. "Well, hurry up and get undressed. We can't wash you and your clothes at the same time!" she laughed.

Seeing another Felis naked was... strange. Astra worried that the body she'd created wasn't normal as she stripped her stiff, stinky shirt off. But Rita didn't seem to notice anything off and instead kept chattering away. "Here's where we keep the soap and towels. We've got people who do nothing but the laundry and clean the bathhouse but try not to make a mess."

She turned the water on and filled a bucket, setting it

next to a bench. "Let's start with your hair. I bet it's so pretty when it's clean. What a shame that you got dragged through the mud."

"I was a corpse for a day and a half," Astra admitted. "Fell into a stream and dragged down the mountain."

Rita paused. "That sounds horrible..." she whispered.

"I wasn't aware of most of it," Astra said and smiled. "But zero-of-ten, do not recommend."

Rita poured cold water on Astra's head, making her yelp, then followed with soap. "We'll wash that memory out along with the muck!" she announced. "And then we'll brush-brush-brush!" The Felis was careful around Astra's ears, though she did take a moment to peer into them.

"Looking for my brains?" Astra asked. "Probably won't find any." Feeling a little embarrassed about someone helping her wash, Astra took the soap and started scrubbing at the rest of her body, then got down to her tail. There were sticks and leaves in the matted fur and she wasn't looking forward to getting that out.

Rita giggled. "I was checking that you didn't catch anything in them. Sorry if that was a little forward. We're used to making sure everyone's healthy when we bathe together. Part of why we bathe together."

"Makes sense..." Astra said. "I don't know much about being Felis... It's just the body I'm in right now."

"Oh! What's your real body like?" Rita asked. "If you had one, that is."

"I do. I was taller. And scrawny. I like this body better."

Rita leaned around to look at her face. "Well. I bet you were pretty either way."

"Not really," Astra said. "I'm much cuter now. But I'm

not used to having ears and a tail that move on their own."

"Well, then, I'll let you in on a few secrets," Rita said. "Try not to sit on your tail. It goes numb quick. And don't let boys pull it."

Astra laughed.

"I was wondering..." Astra said after a little longer. "How many people live here? I haven't seen many Felis."

"There aren't that many of us," Rita said. "There are only forty-five. All the Elves died. The last one just this past fall. She fell out of a tree and broke her neck." Rita piled soap on Astra's head. "There are about fifty-thousand people living here. Mostly Lycanth and Human. It really sucks not having many Felis around because we all end up having to share the same guys and I don't like any of them."

"Why not interbreed?" Astra asked.

"What?"

"Like... have babies with a Human?"

Rita leaned around to look at her. "Are you kidding?" She folded her ears down. "You're not kidding. We can't. That's why," she said. "Felis can only have babies with another Felis. Lycanth can only have babies with other Lycanth. Same with Humans and Elves. That's why all the Elves are gone. Teal was her own cousin several times over. We did what we could to keep her safe, but she just got distracted by all kinds of things. Next thing we knew she was in a tree."

"How old was she?" Astra asked.

"Twenty-nine."

Astra bit her lips together and didn't ask anything more.

Getting her clean took much less time than she was expecting with two of them working on it, but she was surprised she wasn't bald by the time they got her tail brushed out.

Clean and in laundered clothes, Astra realized that she felt a million times better, and followed Rita out of the bathhouse.

"Do you know how to cook?" Rita asked as they approached another building in the opposite direction from the bathhouse. The kitchens were a building that had three stone walls and one wooden one that folded aside, leaving it open to the street.

It was a pleasant temperature inside with the woodburning stoves going. There was a Human woman, who looked around fifty with long, dark hair tied in a tail down her back. She was already at work chopping some vegetables.

"Some," Astra admitted. "I have Chef Skill up to three hundred, but without my Menu, I can't Craft meals."

"That's no problem, dear," the Human woman said. "I'm White." The woman handed over an apron instead of offering her hand. "What kinds of foods do Immortals eat?" she asked.

Astra looked around. "You've got the ingredients for steamed buns," she said when she spotted the wooden bowl of proofed dough. "We would just need to make the filling. There's Boar from last night still, right?"

"Oh yeah! We were going to make that into a stew," Rita said excitedly and pulled Astra over to the pot to look at the beginnings of the stew.

Taking a taste of the stew, Astra nodded. "We can

combine them to make steamed buns. It's good easy to transport food." Her next problem would be the basket in which to steam them.

Searching through the kitchen, she finally came up with a pot and basket situation. "Improvisation. Hope it works!" Astra said.

She then showed White and Rita how to make the dough circles and fold the buns. All three waited impatiently for the first batch of buns to finish, but once they did, they each tried one. Astra fully expected failure, only to be surprised when it was amazing. Excited by the new recipe, White and Rita started rolling out more dough circles and Astra filled them, setting up an assembly line of buns in two steamers.

Then Xander appeared, looking disheveled but alert.

Feelings welled up in her again at seeing his face. Deciding she didn't want to deal with them, she instead gave him some buns and sent him away.

"He is such a stud!" Rita said and giggled. "You're so lucky." The redheaded Felis swished her tail excitedly. "I don't know if I'd be able to control myself if that was tucking me into bed."

Astra flushed and went back to folding filling into the dough.

"Thank you so much for helping make breakfast," White said, "These are amazing. What level is your Chef Skill?"

"Just over three hundred," Astra said.

"Wow! You put some work into that!" Rita enthused.

Flushing again, she looked away shyly. "I like Crafting," she admitted.

"If only we could hog her all day," the younger Felis women lamented.

"She's got to work on the Skills she got yesterday, Rita." White shook her head. "Speaking of which, I see Glen on her way now."

The tabby Felis smiled at Astra as she entered. "You ready to get started leveling your new Skills?"

"Yeah," Astra said and took another steamed bun.

Glen took one as well and bit into it, her ears popping up in surprise. "Wow, this is amazing!"

"You made these?" Glen asked in astonishment.

"Behold!" Rita said, displaying a steamed bun with enthusiasm. "Level three hundred steamed buns!"

"Three hundred?" Glen demanded, her ears folding back. "That's a lot of time you could have been using to level more useful Skills."

"Now Glen, don't yell at her," White admonished.

Glen shook her head. "We're heading out to the forest now. We don't have much time to waste." Taking Astra's arm, she pulled her out of the communal kitchen and towards the trees up the slope.

With little choice, Astra stumbled after the woman.

Once in the trees, she released Astra's wrist, but only because the path upwards wasn't wide enough to continue dragging her. "That man with you. What's his name?"

"Xander," Astra said.

"He seems rather cold, doesn't he?"

Shrugging, Astra said, "Yeah..."

"Why keep him around?"

"He's pretty to look at," Astra admitted. "And I can't make him leave."

Glen abruptly stopped, turning to face Astra. "You have no feelings for him?"

Flustered, Astra picked her nails, feeling her ears going up and down as her tail twitched nervously. "I—uh... well...no?"

The woman sighed. "You should work on hardening your heart. Men like that will only hurt you."

Folding her ears down, Astra frowned. "True..."

"Come. We've no time to waste." Glen started climbing the slope again.

* * *

It felt amazing to be clean and fed. Once he was dressed again, he took his smelly armor out of the bathhouse with him and headed back to the kitchens. The two women from before were there, but not Astra. "Where's Astra gone?" he asked.

"Glen took her for training," the younger woman said.

Xander consulted his directional sense. She was up the mountain by a mile, but her health was fine. He nodded and turned, heading towards the weapons master's place.

Entering the courtyard, he found the old man working on cleaning Astra's armor. Approaching, Xander sat down across from him and took one of the brushes and soap.

"This is some fine armor," the man said. "I've never seen such quality before."

"Astra made it," Xander said as he got to scrubbing the lake and mud out of the leather. The quality was the only reason why it wasn't absolutely destroyed.

"Tell me about the world?" the old man asked.

Xander glanced up to find the man wistfully staring at him. "Of course," he said. "I've been to Aesir, Vanaheim, and Nifelheim. Which city would you like to know about first?"

"Oh—ah... Aesir."

"Aesir is built along the northern shoreline and a nearby island. It is the city of water, sheltered by Leviathan. There are approximately five hundred thousand people living in the city proper and another hundred thousand scattered across the farmlands beyond."

The poor man's jaw had dropped. "I couldn't... imagine that many people!"

Xander smiled. "Aesir is one of the larger population centers," he said. "There are smaller villages scattered around the forest between Aesir and Nifelheim, beneath Vanaheim. Aesir's biggest draws are the aqueducts and fountains, the early architects adored columns and marble, thus the public buildings have one or both of these aspects."

The man sighed, closing his eyes. "I dreamed of getting to see the outside world... I'd dreamed of becoming strong enough to get through the forest and mountains and find out what the rest of the world had gotten up to."

"Perhaps it is still possible," Xander said, although he wasn't sure how. It would be a major undertaking to make a safe path through the Dark Mountains to the closest population center. However, now that Astra had attuned to this Soul Stone, getting back and forth would be that much easier for him and Astra.

"Tell me of the others!" the old man asked.

"Vanaheim, the city of Air rests in the hands of Caelum,"

Xander said. "Is suspended upon floating islands over the forest. It is the ancestral home of the Elves and Avians. The population is also somewhere near five hundred thousand, though I haven't been there in some time. Their architecture consists of trees bent and hollowed out. The great roots hold the floating islands together and serve as roads for those without wings."

"Do people fall off?" the old man asked in wonder. Despite his distraction, his hands were still moving, working the dirt out of the various straps of Astra's armor.

"Occasionally, but safety nets have been installed to prevent anyone from reaching the ground below," Xander said. "Nifelheim, Terra's city of ice and mountain has two levels and each distinct from the other. The actual population is uncountable. Estimates place it around eight hundred thousand."

The man's hands stopped. "Uncountable?" he gasped.

"There are so many tunnels and the Kobolds do not understand the concept of numbers. Asking them to self-report how many of them there are in a warren is... asking too much," Xander said. "The city above is coated in ice, as the chilly winds have set frost upon the walls of buildings for eons, burying any original stonework in meters of ice. The glacier has grown so much over time that the original streets of the city above often count as part of the city below. New buildings of ice are built atop as needed, but only the Giants have the ability to resist the bitter cold and thus prefer to live there, as opposed to the underground where the Dwarves and Kobolds make their home.

"The city below is as brightly lit as Aesir on a clear

day, despite being below the mountain. Their cavern ceilings stretch hundreds of meters high, every surface carved with ancient Dwarven artwork. The city center is a warren of structures built of stones hewn from the living earth, creating a confusing maze should you wish to go into the residential section. There are tunnels that expand further into the mountains and below, wherein the Kobolds make their nests."

Xander smiled slightly at the old man's wonder.

* * *

"Glen—I can't—anymore—" Astra said, collapsing to her knees. She had successfully gotten Elemental Mastery past level fifty and started on Fire Bomb. That was level twenty-five, but she was exhausted, her stomach eating her from the inside.

"Get up and quit being lazy!" Glen shouted. "Worthless excuse for a hero."

Folding down and dropping to her side in the leaves, Astra sighed. Her time sense said it was only a little past noon.

"I believe it is time for a short break," Xander said.

Glen turned, "How did you find us?" she asked, her tone changing immediately to one of cheery sweet.

Astra closed her eyes with a mental sigh. Glen was one of *those* types. All morning, Astra had suffered under the woman's constant demands that she keep going. Faster! What's wrong with you, I thought you were an Immortal. Pitiful excuse. I bet you're not actually an Immortal at all. We all just wasted our Scrolls on you.

"I am always aware of Astra's location," Xander said and stopped beside her.

Keeping her eyes closed, Astra fully expected him to nudge her with his foot. Instead, he crouched next to her. "Eat," he said, holding something that smelled amazing in front of her nose.

Eyes popping open, she focused on the wrapped thing. It smelled like fish and bread with spices, but she had no idea what it was called. Reaching up, she took it and sat up to eat. The food wasn't as high-quality as Astra usually made it, but it was handmade, which made it taste amazing.

"Master Harvey and I cleaned your armor," Xander said. "We shall work on one of the martial Skills next."

"Ughh," Astra mumbled into her food.

"Xander," Glen said, "I was wondering, what Skills do you have?"

"Healer Class," Xander responded. He stood.

"What levels?"

"Cure is my highest over one hundred thousand."

Glen squeaked in disbelief. "H-how?"

"I am over five hundred years old," Xander said blandly.

Astra snorted. "You acted old when you were nineteen."

He cleared his throat in embarrassment but didn't deny it.

Finishing the last bite of her fish wrap, Astra climbed to her feet and stretched. "Okay."

Xander made a few gestures and produced her leather armor from his Inventory. Taking it, Astra pulled the pieces on and buckled them in place. She wasn't really used to donning her armor manually, so it took a minute. He then pulled a spear from his Inventory and held it out to her. "Master Harvey suggested going through the basic motions of attacking and defending first."

Nodding, Astra took the spear and turned to face one of the trees nearby, choosing it as her target. The rock she'd been targeting was blasted to glass and Astra didn't want to destroy the spear tip with a rock.

Stilling her mind in order to access the new Skill set, Astra felt it web together with the Dodge Skill she'd gotten from a Player Scroll.

Lunging forward, she struck the tree, then flowed into another move to strike from a different angle. Five more strikes and she saw the notification of leveling up in her peripheral.

Unfortunately, Glen was not going to leave. She instead moved to stand next to Xander, her tawny tail flicking with interest. She wasn't looking at Astra at all. "Five hundred years," she mused. "I can't imagine how boring that would be."

"I kept busy," Xander said.

"Oh? Doing what?"

"Clergy."

His curt answers were not going to deter the Cougar Karen. "Clergy? Every Elf I've known has been an amazing archer or rogue," Glen said.

"Your exposure to Elves has been limited," Xander pointed out. "Besides, I was chosen by a Healer, thus the Skills I received were from the Healer Class."

[Dragoon Level 2]

Astra tried not to feel jealous of Glen trying to cozy up to Xander. Considering Xander wasn't entertaining it in any form. He just stood there with his arms crossed, watching the woods.

"Tell me- how did you get chosen?" Glen asked.

"You would have to ask Astra about that. It was her choice, after all."

Astra hid her snort of laughter with a thrust of her spear and jumped back briefly in order to make a high jump and attack from above. Landing, she bounced on her toes and stepped back to breathe for a second. She remembered choosing him. She'd spent a week in and out of the Vanaheim Adventurer's Guild, watching the various NPCs that handled posting jobs on the board, cleaning up the public rooms, and serving food and drink. While Players didn't require food to live, they could eat it for stat buffs. It tasted like eating in a dream. Drinking alcohol did create a drunk-like effect. She'd sat at a table in the middle a majority of the time. Most players liked hanging at the edges to look all mysterious. Astra didn't care and just took over a table and did her crafting while she watched the NPCs. The eight-foot-tall Elven boy with silvery hair, pale skin, and deft movements was absolutely the prettiest one in the joint. There were other Elves, of course. The women did their best to advertise their chests and butts to the male Players.

At the time, Astra had thought it was just part of the programming. But now that she knew they'd been people all along, it was actually a good sales tactic. They did receive the most tips and got picked most often.

Xander had approached her a few times over those

few days, asking if she wanted something to eat or drink, his impassive stare an obvious "do not actually ask me for anything" look. It had amused her to no end. His shirt had water spots on it and his sleeves rolled up. Obviously, he was not one of the normal servers, so why was he out asking if she, and only she, wanted anything? Then another Warrior Class had approached Xander while he was at the bar, filing an order with the kitchen and Astra couldn't just let someone else have him. She got up, went to the Porter Hiring counter, and told them who she wanted.

[Dragoon Level 5]

The first batch of levels was always the easiest to get. Getting beyond level twenty would be the slog. She'd need to go out hunting actual monsters to make better progress.

"Do you have any siblings?" Glen asked.

"No."

Astra went through the motions, slowly hacking the tree. If she intended to cut the tree down with a spear, it was going to take a long time. Part of why she'd chosen this thick trunk. It also was a pretty big target, making it harder to miss. Use of a Skill only counted if you hit your intended target.

"What about other family?" Glen asked.

"No."

"No?" Glen asked. "What does that mean?"

"I do not wish to talk about that subject," Xander said.

"I suppose they would have all passed by now," Glen said sympathetically.

Xander did not respond. He would not rise to the bait. Instead, he said, "[Shelter]," casting on Astra. "Razor Boar to the north."

Astra switched her target and went for the live one, it would be worth far more experience if she could kill it with her spear.

* * *

[Dragoon Level 30]

[Elemental Master Level 50]

[Fire Bomb Level 24]

Xander considered the day a success all around. Astra lay in the leaves, wheezing after her second Boar kill of the day. It had taken her hours to whittle them down. He'd had to cast [Stop] to make sure they didn't run away in irritation at being needled to death. If only he could've done the same to Glen. She was determined to needle Xander to death with her overly obvious attempts at flirting and prying at his past. He had little interest in sharing any of that.

Overhead, the sky was turning violet as night set in. More dangerous monsters would be coming out. Xander took Astra's spear, putting it into his Inventory before he rolled her over.

She moaned. It may have been a "leave me alone" but Xander chose to ignore that. Pulling her arms, he sat her up, then hoisted her over his shoulder.

"Noo," she said louder. "I'm not a potato sack..." The weak flail of her arms did no physical damage, although her hand encountered his butt. He tried to ignore it; his ears went hot anyway. Adjusting her, he started walking down the mountain.

"Well, since you won't answer any of my questions

about you," Glen said. "I'll tell you about myself."

"Please don't," Xander said, interrupting. Their feet crunched through the fallen leaves and sticks that littered the ground beneath the canopy.

Glen, stunned to silence, flapped her mouth.

"I have to listen for monsters," Xander said to smooth the woman's fur. He'd gotten sick of her questions hours ago. The only respite was when monsters wandered close enough for Astra to target and the time it took her to whittle them down.

"We're within range of Vard's guards," Glen said.

"Didn't stop two Razor Boars from approaching," Xander pointed out. "Something more powerful could easily break through and attack."

"If it does, we're all doomed anyway," Glen muttered.

"You have a high-powered Healer here," Xander pointed out. "And Astra is capable of raising Undead on a much higher level than I can."

"She's exhausted," Glen pointed out.

"I don't have to be awake for my Undead to do what they're called for," Astra said, mumbling against Xander's back. She'd stopped fighting.

Glen seemed perturbed, perhaps she'd forgotten Astra was there. Her ears flicked down, then up again as she put her sultry smile back on. At least she shut up, but she did walk incredibly close beside him, opposite the shoulder Astra dangled from. Reaching the bottom, White ran up to meet them. "Is she dead?" she asked.

"Exhausted. Is there food available?" Xander asked.

"Of course!" The woman hurried off immediately. Xander continued towards the house he and Astra had been given. Glen split off to head elsewhere. He glanced over, catching her lashing her tail, ears laid back in irritation. Entering the house, Xander paused in surprise at the new bed. It was much larger than the one that had been there previously. It took up much of the single small room and had been piled with blankets. Lowering Astra to the bed, he let her fall out across it and found himself kneeling over her, her hands above her head, eyes closed but lips slightly parted. Her short white hair framed her face in a fluffy bob.

Xander gently brushed away a strand from where it clung to the corner of her mouth.

The knock on the door interrupted his thoughtless staring and Xander pushed off the bed to greet the cook. She'd brought stew for both Astra and him. "Thank you," he said.

"You'd better watch out for Glen," White said, "She's on the hunt for a new plaything and I think she's taken an interest in you."

Xander shook his head with a slight smile. "Disappointment is all that awaits her," he said.

The woman laughed. "Good. Glad she won't get her way for once." She retreated and left Xander to shut the door with his foot. Returning to the bed, he set one bowl down on the floor in favor of gently shaking Astra awake.

"Huh?"

"Eat," he said and helped her sit up before handing her the bowl. She grumbled at the movement but ate her stew quickly. Sitting on the floor beside the bed, Xander picked up his own bowl of stew and leaned back against the wall to eat.

Finishing her bowl, Astra stood from the bed, stretched, and began fumbling with the buckles of her armor. Peeling herself out of the leathers, she dropped them on the floor at the foot of the bed. Then the clothes she wore under the armor followed. Bare as the day she was born, she climbed into bed.

Xander stared, stew forgotten in his mouth. Once she'd covered up, he closed his eyes and forced himself to swallow.

* * *

She woke to the early morning light again. This time, Xander was curled against her back, face against her shoulder, his arm around her. A layer of blanket separated them, but that wasn't much when she realized she was naked.

Face burning, Astra couldn't bring herself to move.

Xander did, though. Sighing softly in his sleep and putting his face against the nape of her neck. His hips pressed against the pillow between them.

She knew nothing had happened. In fact, she suspected she'd undressed herself. He'd been an absolute gentleman and laid on top of the blankets. Reaching back, she checked, finding that he was even wearing pants, as she'd suspected. She had been the indecent one.

Ears folding down, she just wanted to die. Her fingers clutched the blanket, eyes stinging. If this had been back on Earth, she knew it wouldn't have ended well. Xander was... so... she couldn't understand his patience or his self-restraint when it came to her. He had so much power

over her right now and he wasn't using it.

"Nothing happened," Xander said and sat up, avoiding looking at her.

"I know... I just... can't believe I did that..." Astra pulled the blanket over her face.

"You were exhausted," Xander said and slid off the opposite side of the bed. He shuffled around a moment, and she felt cloth hit the bed next to her.

Still unable to look at him, she curled into a ball, pulling the pillow over her head too.

"Don't wallow in embarrassment too long. You have much to do," Xander said and left.

Astra peeled the pillow off when she was sure he was gone and sat up. He'd left her shirt and pants from the day before on the bed. Her underwear remained somewhere in the pile of armor on the floor. Climbing out of the bed, she straightened the blankets, still feeling like her face would melt from blushing. Picking through the discarded equipment, she found what she needed and put them on. If she'd had her Inventory, she would have just equipped them instead of having to deal with all the hooks and straps.

Picking up her armor, she headed to the bathhouse to get a quick wash before assisting White and Rita with breakfast. When she arrived at the kitchens, she found the two women butchering the Boars from yesterday.

"Hey," she greeted. "Sorry, those are such a mess..."

"They're good stew meat," White said. "Help us out, though?"

"Right." Astra rolled up her sleeves and approached.

As she worked, Astra assessed her physical condition

and determined that she felt fine. She didn't feel delirious or like her brain was shutting down. She kind of felt refreshed. Surely her body on Earth was dying by now. Or had she been found? Were they taking care of her? Why was she still in Ashguard then? Getting the VR headset knocked off would only result in disorientation, rather than brain damage. Surely, they would've tried to wake her up if they'd found her...

Her hands moved automatically as she thought, cutting the Boar open at specific points to drain blood into a bucket and gut it.

She'd given up thinking this was some kind of update to the world that made it a single-player game. If that had been the case, there would've been side quests and stuff instead of just the Convergence plot line. Were the fail-safes on her headset turned off then? Was that why she felt like she was actually here in Ashguard? Surely there wasn't a real world that had pocket dimensions that kept meals hot and steaming right next to frozen treats, cold as the day they were freshly made for as long as they were in your Inventory. Surely this world wasn't real.

Xander's face was far too pretty for him to have been simply born with it. It had to be computer-generated.

So why couldn't she log out?

"Wow! That's... the best cuts of meat I've ever seen," Rita said.

Astra blinked back to the situation at hand and found that she'd nearly finished tearing down the Boar. Everything usable was off it and set out in an orderly fashion. Targeting it, she read the text popup: [Pork Belly Level 334, Crafter Astra Diane]. She'd successfully used her Crafting Skill without using her Menu. Despite the pig having been tormented to death, the meat would undoubtedly still taste good due to her high Skill used when butchering it.

Did that mean she didn't need her Menu to access her Crafting Skills? If they worked the same as a combat Skill, she just had to remember what she could do and just... do it.

...Did that mean she might not need her Menu at all?

* * *

Xander was extremely glad that Astra had covered her face when he got up. Knowing that she'd seen his raging erection would have been the end of his self-restraint. He'd shoved a pillow between them to keep from grinding it into her during the night. When she reached back and touched his hip, he had to bite his lip and hold his breath. He was quick to get up, tossing Astra's shirt and pants onto the bed before escaping to get to the bathhouse.

Thankfully no one was there, which allowed him the chance to quietly dispose of his load down the drain. With post-cum clarity, he realized he should not have gotten into the bed with her at all last night and this situation was his own fault. Next time she did that, he would sleep on the floor, he told himself.

Not that it helped right now. Finishing his wash, Xander got dressed and headed out to see if anything had gone wrong overnight. He had acquainted himself with the hunters that guarded Vard. There weren't many of them, but they were highly Skilled, having learned their abilities the natural way. They carried a great many scars, but they also had stories. Getting to know them felt a lot like being back in Hollowood, except he was marginally more respected here. Not trusted, but respected as a Healer.

Approaching the lead hunter, Xander lifted his hand in greeting.

The Human woman nodded in return.

"Any trouble last night?" he asked.

"No," she said. Most of her forces were Lycanth, the remainder were Humans with a few Felis and Giants. She moved on, leaving him to his thoughts as she went to the bathhouse. Letting her go, Xander continued through the city, learning his way around and taking stock of the inhabitants.

There were very few Felis in the small city, he'd noticed, and no Elves. There were Dwarves and Giants in Vard as well, but they all had an air of depression as if they were just waiting to die off. He supposed it made sense. If Vard had been isolated for so long and most of the population had been killed in the last Convergence, what remained was likely not going to last much longer. Xander, being Elven, couldn't contribute. Astra… well, it was a question as to whether an Immortal could bear children.

In effect, they were both essentially useless for the longevity of Vard. Although, Astra could bring new people if they were willing now that she'd attuned to the Soul Stone. If she could safely get back to one of the major cities.

Kayson's warning still rang in Xander's head.

Immortals could make new Soul Pacts with

Ashguardians after their previous one died, and their soul left. Ashguardians, however, were stuck for life. Xander would have to die in order to allow someone else to make a Pact with her. He had no intention of dying permanently for someone else's potential gain. Not that they would gain much more than access to Unlocked Healer Skills. Every other Cursed One in the world had Warrior or Mage Class.

The more he thought about it, the stupider it seemed. Hopefully, others would come to that conclusion soon.

His stomach reminded him that he hadn't eaten breakfast yet, and Astra had probably helped prepare the food, meaning it would be high-quality.

Xander swallowed, having salivated at the thought.

Heading back towards the communal kitchens, he was in time to see Astra giving the local children baked goods. He smiled to himself at that. She'd always had a soft spot for children, it seemed. Even when she couldn't understand what anyone was saying, she would automatically step in whenever a child was in danger. The street urchins in all three major cities flocked to her whenever word got around that she was in town because she would always feed them. She fed the homeless too, whenever she saw them.

Xander supposed that was ultimately why he loved her.

If he was being entirely honest with himself… it was why he'd joined the Guild after being let go by Walter at the Item Store. She probably didn't even remember, but he had been one of the people she just gave food to once. Sure, he'd been employed at the time, but he'd been standing outside a tavern, mentally calculating if he had enough money to get more than a loaf of bread when she'd tapped his arm and handed him a meal.

He'd seen her before. He'd heard the other kids talking about the Immortal that gave out food.

That had been the first time he'd ever seen her up close.

After that, Walter's shop had closed and Xander decided to try his luck at becoming an Assistant.

Shaking his head, he pushed the memories away and approached the kitchens. Astra saw him coming, flushed with embarrassment, but still gave him a bowl of stew and a hunk of bread. "I was going to try to get my Menu out of the lake with Undead today," she said.

Xander nodded as he ate, leaning against the door frame of the kitchen as he listened to her.

"I can use my Hunter and Cooking Skills without my Menu at least," she said and went back to helping Rita and White make more food for the city.

If nothing else, this seemed like the perfect setting for her, Xander supposed. He swallowed. "Did you not realize that before?" he asked.

She turned to look up at him, ears folding back. "No." Astra glared. "I'm guessing you did, and you didn't say anything."

"I thought you knew," Xander mused.

"Well, assume I don't notice stuff," Astra grumbled. "I've got a lot going on right now."

"I will keep that in mind," he said, lingering over his breakfast. "When would you like to attempt the retrieval?"

"When I'm done here," Astra said.

"You can go whenever. You've already helped so much," Rita said. She grinned at Xander as she wiped her hands off and went to shoo Astra out of the kitchen. "Go take a walk on the beach before Glen gets here!" She took the ladle from Astra's hand. "Go on! We'll be fine!"

Summarily ejected, Astra pouted slightly, then took off her apron and hung it up before turning to head down the slope towards the sparkling water. Xander followed, still eating. He would return the bowl later. It wasn't like it took up much space in his Inventory.

Astra's tail swayed behind her as she walked. It was back to its lustrous fluffiness. He wanted to pet it. Maybe she'd let him do so later.

Reaching the shore, Astra folded her arms, pushing her large breasts up as she squinted at the water.

Dropping her hands, she cast, "[Raise Undead]." The hundred shambling hoards pushed up from the ground, rotting flesh dripping off them as they got to their feet and stood waiting for a command. They were never clothed, their noses and genitals the most rotten parts on them. Xander supposed that was the worst part about them. He looked away and hurried to finish eating.

Astra pointed at the water, silently telling her monstrous army to go forth.

They shambled into the gently lapping waves, sloshing ever deeper until the bottom dropped out a hundred feet in.

A fin broke the surface of the water further out. A great tail slapped the water closer, then the water began churning.

Astra folded her arms again. "They're getting eaten,"

she said. "I'm just chumming the water at this point."

"Wonder if lake monster tastes any good," Xander said and glanced down at her.

Her fingers tapped on her arm, and her bright green eyes narrowed. "Lake Monster Sushi? I'm down to try it."

"It seems only fair," Xander added. "They tried to eat you a few days ago."

"Then it's settled. I'll hunt lake monster next." Astra fell silent a moment. "And that's the last of my hoard. Mission failed." She turned to look up at Xander fully. "I've been thinking. You Ashguardians have a way to make Scrolls without a Menu. How do you do it?"

"I focus on a Skill as if checking its level," Xander said thoughtfully. He focused on his Cure Skill and reached out. "Then I pull..." he pulled the edge of the window he could see, and the Scroll unfurled into reality. He looked down at Astra.

"I'll give it a try," she said. "We need to find an alternative if I can't get my Menu back. What am I supposed to see when I focus on the Skill?"

"Writing in the air, within a blue frame," Xander gestured with his hands to describe its size.

She stared at him. "And... your people have always been able to do this?"

Xander nodded. "Why? You can too?"

"Only when I'm in Ashguard. Or some other game. People from my world can't see stuff like that normally." Astra's brows knit. "From what Ruth said, the whole Skill Scroll thing has been around for a long time." She looked up at him. "You're absolutely sure your world is real?" she asked.

Feeling uncomfortable, Xander looked out at the lake instead of at her as he thought about it. Admittedly it was suspicious that someone could don a crown and transport themselves into a body they deliberately created to interact with another world. Additionally, while Skills were convenient, learning something the old-fashioned way would make that person a Skill Master, which implied that something had tampered with the way the world worked to make it possible to easily share Skills.

If, as the Holy Writ said, sharing Skills was the way they were supposed to prepare for a Convergence... wasn't it strange how the people of the world were capable of doing that in the first place? That it was a system that the Immortals- no, the Players, had taken to as if it was how they expected Ashguard to function? Perhaps they were right and Xander was wrong.

He glanced back at Astra to find her squinting at the air. She pressed her fingers to her temples in concentration.

Astra held her breath, cheeks puffing out. "Phyahh! I'm not seeing any windows. I'll keep trying later," she said. "Maybe I can do it next time I level a Skill up. Speaking of which, let's head out to hunt something." She stared at the water for a second before turning her back on it and heading towards the mountain. She apparently wasn't ready for swimming so soon in the day.

Xander followed. He hoped that Glen would not be joining them.

When they reached the path up the mountain, his hopes were dashed, for there she stood, arms folded and frowning. "I was wondering if she was going to skip training today," Glen said.

155

"No, I was feeding the lake monsters," Astra retorted.

"Why would you want to feed them?"

"I didn't. I wanted my minions to explore the lake and look for my Menu, but the lake monsters thought my minions were food," Astra explained. "In any case, today, I'm going to hunt more monsters to level up my Skills since Xan will be there to cast Shelter. You don't have to escort me today. I appreciate your help yesterday."

Glen put on a curdled smile. "I need to make sure you make good use of the Skills I gave you," she said. Her smile turned sweeter when she cast it on Xander.

He could see right through it to her rotten core.

Chapter 5

[Dragoon Level 51]

[Fire Bomb Level 50]

[Ice Flash Level 34]

Astra stumbled along behind Glen and Xander. She'd kept her feet this time around by focusing on her melee leveling in the morning and magic in the afternoon. She was still exhausted and having trouble keeping upright on the uneven terrain.

Ahead, Glen hopped down a four-foot rock ledge. Xander dropped down it easily as well. They both kept going, but when Astra came to it, she realized that dropping down the way they had would drop her. She also knew that if she sat down to slide off the drop, she'd never get back up and glanced left and right in the growing darkness. Neither direction offered a better solution.

She squatted down and braced her hands on the rock to turn and drop her feet over the edge.

Arms swept her up before her toes touched the ground.

Folding her ears, she looked up at Xander as he lifted her easily. "I can walk," she said.

"It will be full dark by the time you get down the mountain by yourself," Xander said. He did not put her down. Embarrassed by Glen's forced smile as the older Felis waited for them to join her, Astra ended up putting her head down and instead tried to focus on her Skills.

She'd almost had it earlier, she thought. *But no cigar.*

Astra dropped her head against Xander's shoulder,

exhausted, although perhaps not as exhausted as the day before. Doing Mage Skills felt different than doing Healer Skills. It was like she was accessing a completely different muscle, the same way doing Warrior Skills felt like different muscles than just jogging around everywhere the way she used to.

Glen took up talking again. "I learned all the Mage Skills from my father. It took years to master them. You see, to make a Master Scroll, we must get the Skill the hard way, learning day by day. None of this," Glen gestured vaguely, "leveling up and instantly having access. I had to start learning when I was five how to pull the mana from the air and turn it into fire in my hands." She paused for a second. Astra didn't bother opening her eyes to see that she was being glared at, she already knew.

"The Skill Scrolls are important for passing on knowledge quickly in times of need," Xander said. "We do not have the time to train everyone in every Skill from the ground up."

"Time," Glen snorted. "I think it's all Boar holloks."

"The stars are in alignment with the Plaques in your temple," Xander pointed out. "Yet you deny a Convergence is soon upon us?"

"I just think that it's something that happened a long time ago and isn't likely to happen again," Glen said.

"Head in the sand," Astra said.

"What?" Glen asked.

"Everyone always thinks that the worst things can't happen because it hasn't happened to them. And then bam, you get hit by lightning because you could've taken basic precautions, but you thought you were invincible."

Glen remained silent. "So you believe this calamity is coming too?" she asked.

"Whether it is or isn't, I've got your Skills and will level them up in order to hand them out to everyone," Astra said. "If it looks like rain, wear a raincoat." Prying an eye open, she looked at Glen. The woman was openly wearing her distaste for Astra in front of Xander. Maybe the old cougar had given up trying to get in his pants. He clearly wasn't interested.

"I still don't believe you're Immortal," Glen stated.

"Okay," Astra said and shrugged. Astra felt Xander almost laugh but choke it down.

Coming into the lights of the village, Xander stopped by the kitchen, letting Rita hand Astra a couple of bowls of Boar stew before he headed on to their borrowed house.

This time, I will not strip in front of him! Astra promised herself. At the door, Xander set her feet on the ground and took one of the bowls from her, instead, he took a seat on the narrow porch across the front of the house. "It's a nice evening," he said, kicking his feet out.

Astra's thighs trembled as she bent down to sit and collapsed at the last inch. "I'm not going to be able to get up," she said and started eating tiredly.

"I'll carry you."

Her ears flicked. "You've been carrying me a lot lately," she pointed out.

"I could leave you on the mountain." He said the words, but his tone was not serious. "But that would break my promise."

Astra glanced up at him with a slightly raised eyebrow.

Xander's spoon paused partway to his mouth. "To not

leave you alone at night."

"Why, though?"

"Why?"

"Why promise that?" She looked away. "I'm an adult. It's not like I haven't slept alone for years. Just because you never saw me sleep before recently doesn't mean I can't do it by myself."

His palm contacted her hair, then caressed along her ear. Unable to help it, she leaned into the touch. As a Human, she still wasn't quite used to having these extra appendages. Her tail occasionally had a mind of its own and flopped around whenever she was angry or agitated, betraying her state of mind. "That may be true, but you haven't ever spent over twenty-four hours at the edge of death."

A chill swept through her. The cold reminder of that emptiness that chewed at the edges of her soul until barely anything remained made her shiver. "I'm fine," she said.

"Hmm," Xander said, obviously not believing her. "Do not lie to me. You wanted to die at that time."

Ears down against her skull, she glared towards the gently glowing Soul Stone. "Maybe. But what's it really matter? Why do you keep bringing this up?"

"Because it concerns me," Xander said. "Over the last few days... I have spent more time reading the Plaques. They imply that this is not the first time your people have come to this world. The Skill Scrolls themselves imply that a system, much like your Menu was in place long before the Players appeared. Something more—deeper— is at work and the gods have a hand in it. My anger at you was misplaced, for it was the other Players who abused the people of this world. You helped people as much as you caused damage." How he still had an appetite with this heavy subject, Astra had no clue. "Eat, before it gets cold."

Reluctantly, Astra shoveled the remainder of her stew into her face.

Xander took her empty bowl, leaving her on the porch as he headed back to the kitchens to return the dishes.

Leaning back on her hands, Astra stared up at the trees and the sparkles of stars between the branches. The weather had been pleasant thus far, but having spent a lot of time in Ashguard, she knew there were seasons. It was early Fall now.

And Xander's words... He felt bad for making her feel bad enough to want to die. Her life had been meaningless on Earth, and now it was just barely above meaningless. She at least could provide Scrolls for people after working her ass off to get the Skills up to level fifty. But past that, what then? She was kind of useless again. In fact, she was entirely useless if she couldn't make the Scrolls in the first place. That was if she even lived past the death of her body on Earth. Surely, she should have died by now. Or at least been close to death. Something should have indicated that she was just lying there unattended for days.

Squinting at the sky, she tried to imagine the Skill Screen, but nothing appeared.

Maybe she was doing it wrong?

"But really. Why do you sleep with me every night?" Astra asked when Xander returned. She cut a look at him. "Is it because you like me?"

"I met a young man," Xander said as he took a seat on

the porch beside her again, "A few years after the Players left. I found him dead on the roadside between Vanaheim and Nifelheim."

Astra closed her mouth.

"I Resurrected him, of course. I wasn't sure how long he had been dead, but the spark of life was fading from his corpse. At first, he seemed confused as to where he was. I assumed he'd been mugged since he had no possessions and no obvious marks of a monster attack." Xander shifted, straightening his back briefly, looking up at the sky. "Once he recovered from the initial confusion and stiffness... He told me he'd attempted to end his own life. He was not pleased to have been brought back."

"Should have minded your own business," Astra mused, guessing where this story was going.

"He was the son of a rich merchant," Xander said giving her a sharp look from the corner of his eye. "He had chosen death rather than submit to a marriage he did not want. I offered a compromise; I would escort him somewhere his family did not have reach and report to his father that I had found him dead. The young man agreed and seemed excited about the prospect of starting a new life. I left him outside of Nifelheim while I went to report the death to his family. When I returned, I found that his soul had left him entirely."

Astra blinked. "But—what?"

"Death does not release its grip so easily once a person has gotten to a certain point. Especially when they eagerly embraced it. I still see Death's Shade in your eyes."

"So, you're not afraid of me killing myself, but of Death just taking me," Astra said and looked away.

"Because you invited it once before," Xander said gently. "I was wrong in my words to you that day."

Astra's ears folded down. He'd said it several times now, so maybe he really meant his apology. She glanced up to find him staring into the distance. It wasn't fair—she was really starting to like him, but she was pretty sure he had no such feelings for her. Yet he was going to continue sleeping with her, keeping her company, keeping her safe...

Either I crush this crush quick... or suffer, she realized.

* * *

Astra remained quiet the rest of the evening. His words must have had an impact on her since she lay awake for quite some time as the quiet of the night settled into Vard.

Xander lay behind her as usual, her tail brushing against his leg as it twitched every now and then.

He'd lied.

He'd neglected to mention that Frou and Baldur had been with him at the time, and it had been Baldur's idea to tell the young man's family the lie, not Xander's. Xander had been too drunk to care. Xander had been there when the young man died anyway. Xander had been too drunk to notice. He'd been passed out until Baldur came back to their camp and got mad.

All that was in the past, though, and Xander now knew the reason the young man had simply died in his sleep. The young man hadn't had enough reason to live and though his body was alive, his soul had still departed. There really wasn't anything Xander could have done even if he'd been sober.

Astra, however, was not in danger of just dying if he left her alone. Since receiving all those Skills and beginning leveling them up, he'd seen the light return to her eyes. She was still depressed. She still had something on her mind that worried her greatly. However, she had something she was living for now, and that was enough to keep her soul attached to her body. Xander's reason for remaining beside her in bed was entirely selfish.

She purred in her sleep sometimes.

He wasn't aware that Felis purred. Isabella certainly hadn't ever done so. But having a warm, soft woman in the bed next to him, gently purring was a bliss he wasn't willing to give up easily. And if he was being honest with himself, Isabella had been a substitute for what he'd really wanted at the time. Now that he had Astra in his arms, he finally understood why Isabella had done what she did. It didn't make her actions right, and it had certainly still hurt tremendously. She'd known well before he did who his heart belonged to.

When he thought about it, the very idea was stupid. He'd been unable to communicate with Astra for eight years, but somehow, he felt as if he'd gotten to know her. Sometimes she had talked at him, animated and upset, or at times, on the verge of tears. He had never doubted that Astra Diane was a living person. He'd always wondered where she went when she disappeared from Ashguard, since her actions when she returned sometimes indicated that her life beyond was frustrating.

Now, knowing that she suffered through a daily grind of living payday to payday, Xander felt even more attached to her. He could protect her from that life, alleviate that stress.

He could rescue her, even while she was fully capable of rescuing him in return.

Almost as if on cue, Astra's purr began to vibrate against his chest.

Xander curled closer against her, putting his face in her hair. Even if he was five hundred, he still had the body of a nineteen-year-old, and he was still a man. It took a lot to keep his hands to himself, but if that was the price he paid for getting to have physical contact with someone who wasn't in absolute awe of him and everything he'd accomplished... well, so be it.

That was another reason he felt attracted to her. She was limitlessly powerful.

Although multiple women in Vard had approached him, he felt above them. He knew that was wrong, too. Just because he was older and much more powerful than any of them could hope to achieve didn't make him better than them, but he still found himself disliking them on that fact alone. They would never achieve what he had. Even if what he'd achieved was only thanks to the woman he was selfishly cuddling.

Her purrs started to fade and Xander lifted a hand to pet her ear, reviving that gentle rumble.

The worst part was that he knew he was arrogant and that his own arrogance was the reason for his loneliness.

Lower my standards and be disappointed in myself or remain forever alone, Xander thought. Well... not forever. He always had the option of dying. Yet after that conversation with Astra, it would be hypocritical of him to take that option. So, he was stuck.

Lying still, listening to Astra's purrs, he let himself relax into sleep.

* * *

Xander had barely moved in his sleep, his arms around her, face against the nape of her neck.

She liked waking up like this and wished that it would be... could be something more. Regardless of the apologies, he'd given for lashing out about the behavior of the Players, she was still one of the ones who perpetuated the crimes against those who lived in Ashguard. She doubted he would ever fully forgive her. From her experience with men, he obviously did not find her attractive, considering he hadn't done anything to her this whole time.

He remained asleep even as she lifted his hand from where it was tucked against her stomach. Fascinated by how tiny her hand was compared to his, she ran her fingers over his palm, admiring the difference in how pale he was compared to her onyx darkness. Xander mumbled against the back of her neck, his lips brushing her skin, fingers curling around hers and pulling her more firmly against him.

"Don't get up," she realized he'd said. Maybe he was just having a good dream about someone else.

In any case, she could hear the village children playing outside, rollicking down the road towards the kitchens. There wasn't any need to get up just yet, Astra decided and relaxed into the warm bed. It was chilly beyond the covers anyway.

She was nearly asleep again when Xander stirred.

"Sleep well?" Astra asked. "I think my tail got a little wild last night..."

"No worse than usual," Xander said and rolled onto his back with a sigh.

Astra sat up and looked back at him. He had one hand under the covers, scratching his stomach. A pillow crease had marked the side of his face. Covering her mouth, she tried not to laugh but snorted instead.

He stared at her in confusion.

"You've got a line on your face," she said. "At least you didn't drool in my hair."

Astra climbed off the bed and went to get her armor, heading towards the bathhouse.

Arriving at the kitchens, Astra found Rita and White already at it with the monster meat Astra had defeated the day before. "I didn't know we could eat tree-squid."

"Oh, no," Rita said. "But the ink sacks are useful. Here, cut them out for me?"

Astra took the knife she was handed and hesitated before picking up one of the squid's legs. This would have been something her crafting Skills could take care of easily, but she wasn't sure how to handle this.

"Stop thinking about it so hard," White admonished.

"Is that how you guys use Skills?"

Rita's ears flicked down. "How do you use Skills?" she asked. "When you're out there hunting these things down?"

"I just..." Astra looked down at the squid again. It was like any other muscle, she could use. Remembering the feeling of using her Alchemy Skill, Astra set her knife to the squid and in three quick cuts had the perfectly undamaged ink sacks out and on the table. Focusing, she rendered the rest of the monster's body into useful components for Alchemy as well and laid them out.

Reaching for her Alchemy Skill again, she felt it come to her. A glimmer in the air—no, a window! With text!

[Alchemy, Level 544]

She grabbed the edge of the window and pulled the way Xander had shown her. The Scroll unfurled into her hand. "Ah!" she shrieked. "Ah! AAAH! I *did it!*" She pulled another and turned to Rita and White. "Here! Here!" she shoved the Scrolls into their hands.

The women stared at her for a moment before breaking into grins. "Alchemy!" Rita gasped. "That'll be useful!"

Astra focused on her Cure Skill. The text appeared.

[Cure, Level 99933]

She pulled two of those and handed them over, followed by two Resurrects, two Regenerations, and two Buffs. "I've got so many Skills and I can only make ten a day!" Astra lamented, then wondered about that. Focusing on another Skill, she tried pulling a Scroll, only for nothing to happen. "Only ten a day still." Clenching her fists, she stared at the floor. *Xander has an Inventory he can access without a Menu. I should be able to do that too!*

How did it feel... to access her Inventory?

Like... opening a pocket, but inside of her.

Sweeping her left hand over the way she'd seen Xander do, she focused her eyes on the pile of things only she could see and was aware of.

"Haven't you eaten yet?" Glen asked irritably.

Astra grinned at her, grasping the mage robes she'd

crafted a while ago and hadn't gotten around to selling. "Here!" she pulled them out and dropped them into Glen's arms.

The Felis woman's ears folded down, then popped up in shock. She remained speechless as Astra hurried past her, pulling out other things for any villagers she passed, upgrading their weapons and armor until she'd emptied her Inventory of any previously made goods.

She caught up with Xander as he stepped out of the bathhouse, combing his hair.

"You look excited," he observed.

Astra, grinning ear to ear, pulled his clergy robes from her Inventory. "I figured it out! I don't need the Menu!" She flung the robes at his face and darted off.

* * *

Xander caught the robes and clutched them in disbelief as Astra sped off. Now that he looked, the other villagers were either holding or wearing items of Astra's Crafting. She had upgraded a good number of people's stuff, making them far more formidable against the local monsters than they had been. Sticking his robes into his Inventory, Xander headed towards the sanctuary where he would find Ruth.

The old Lycanth woman was already outside, speaking with someone who had received one of Astra's Warrior harnesses. The young man was gesturing excitedly while Ruth tried her best to get a look at the item.

"I have a favor to ask," Xander said, addressing them both.

"Oh—Xander! Look! It's amazing!" the hunter said.

"It is. I was going to ask that you make good use of it and bring Astra more crafting materials. As much as you can."

Ruth turned to look up at Xander. "Are you saying she would be willing to outfit the entire village?"

"Yes," Xander said without hesitation. "It will be more difficult to stop her."

"What will she need?" the hunter asked.

"Wood, minerals, leathers, pelts, gems," Xander said. "Anything you think might be useful, just let her have it. If she cannot use it, she will return it."

"What about Skill Scrolls?" Ruth asked.

"She can make ten a day," Xander said.

"Mama Ruth!" a woman shouted as she ran in their direction. "Mama!" Rita called. "I'm a Healer now! Astra gave me a bunch of Healer Skills and Alchemy! They can all go to level one hundred!"

Her shout, along with Astra's gifts soon had practically everyone in the village gathering at the Soul Stone.

Xander used his Direction Sense to find that Astra was being herded towards the center of the crowd and soon joined him where he stood next to Ruth. She was breathless and flushed, eyes bright and ears perked. He couldn't help but smile at her.

Ruth raised her staff and waved it, the rattles on the end drawing everyone's attention and allowing her the silence to speak and be heard. "As you have heard, Astra has been handing out equipment," Ruth said. "She is capable of making more but will need materials. Gather anything you think might be useful and bring it to the sanctuary where it can be sorted. She will begin handing out Skills, ten a day. Anyone under the age of ten will not receive these and will continue to learn a Skill the hard way."

A chorus of groans from young throats went up.

"We must preserve our ability to create Skill Masters for the future," she continued. "That is your duty, younglings. Your sacrifice is vital. We must be prepared for the upcoming Convergence, so begin fortifying your homes and gathering food and water for a long stay in the sanctuary." She waved her staff, shaking the rattle at the top once more and the crowd began dispersing. She pointed at Xander and Astra. "You two, come." She turned, heading back into the sanctuary.

Once inside the cooler darkness, Ruth turned to them and said, "We should decide who will get which Skills. We will not be able to give everyone all your Skills, Astra. There is not enough time."

"Everyone should have Cure, Resurrect, and Regeneration," Xander said flatly.

"Not everyone needs it up to level one hundred," Ruth replied. "You can make Skill Scrolls as well?"

"Yes, they cap at fifty."

"That would be good enough for most of the Warriors," Ruth said and turned to Astra, "Focus on making Scrolls for the Warrior and Mage Skills. These will go to our younger Warriors. Higher healing Scrolls will go to the older Warriors and those unsuited to combat."

Astra lifted a hand. "I think the crafting Skills should be added to that too," she said. "My Chef Skill imbues food I make with buffs. The Tailor, Armorer, and Blacksmith Skills make better armor. Alchemy can be used to make healing potions and other useful items."

"What are your current levels?" Ruth asked.

Astra paused a moment as she focused. "Raise Undead, over ninety-nine thousand, Resurrect, two thousand forty-three. Regeneration, over ninety thousand. Cure, ninety-nine thousand—"

Ruth waved her hand, obviously overwhelmed by those numbers. "Which Skills are not to level fifty yet?"

"Sword and shield, Chakra, Bloodrage, Focus, Bulwark, Taunt, Monk, Bruiser, Dual Wield, Ice Flash, Quagmire, Tangle, Storm, Chaos, Blemish, Dark, and Light," Astra listed along with a number of others that were more specific. "Nearly all the Skills your people gave me. I've got a bunch of Skills that your people didn't have Scrolls for, too. But I think focusing on giving everyone the ability to heal themselves and others is important. You've got a lot of Warriors who have survived this long, they're highly Skilled people just on their own."

Xander nodded, his arms folded as he thought. "Arming them with higher quality gear and the ability to heal and Resurrect would prevent a lot of losses."

"In hoard situations, area effects work well when you've got the enemy bottlenecked," Astra added. "And if we've got a bunch of people with Raise Undead, that'd add to the virtual number of defenders. Especially if they cast in staggered waves."

"Level one hundred doesn't offer much in the way of Undead," Xander said. "It raises ten for fifteen minutes and they aren't very durable. Perhaps Shelter should be a focus instead? It can cover the Soul Stone Plaza for five minutes at level one hundred."

Astra paced away in thought, tail flicking. "Yeah, that would be easier to stagger casting. Does the local wildlife join the fight?" she asked.

Xander looked to Ruth.

Ruth shrugged. "The histories don't say."

"It would still be useful to get rid of the biggest creatures in the area, just to prevent them from attacking the village while it's down." Astra snapped and turned, "Golems! And Summons. Those could help too. They have higher durability than the Undead and last until they're destroyed. If everyone has either or both of those, we can double the population of defenders. And while we're at area effect healing, Buff, Bless, and Sacred Ground would be handy even at level fifty." She looked to Ruth. Xander looked over as well to find the old Lycanth nodding.

"Then focus on creating Scrolls for each of these and leave them in the sanctuary, I shall handle distributing them," Ruth said.

Xander nodded. "In that case, allow me to produce my ten for the day." He focused on his Bless Skill and pulled ten Scrolls, handing them to Ruth. "Ten Bless," he reported. "What have you handed out?"

"Two Alchemy, two Resurrect, two Cure, two Regeneration, two Buff," Astra reported. "All went to Rita and White."

Ruth nodded. "We will give them the rest of the Healer Class Skills at level one hundred."

"And Chef," Astra said. "I'll give them Chef Skill, too."

"In the meantime, they need to level up their new Skills, and so do you," Xander said. "Ruth, instruct all the Warriors to go to the kitchen to receive treatments and buffs before and after they go out hunting. Astra, let us go take care of some of the lake monsters."

Astra nodded. "Okay."

* * *

Much as she disliked the idea of swimming in that murky water, Astra stood on the shore with Xander, getting ready to dive in and kill some lake monsters. At least this time she had access to her Inventory, which meant she could use a water breathing potion. Pulling a couple out, she handed one to Xander. "These will give us five hours underwater," she said.

"It's pretty dark down there," Xander said.

"Got that covered too," Astra said, pulling out two pairs of goggles she'd just crafted, handing one to him. "Goggles of Water Sight."

"You think of everything, don't you?" Xander said, looking amused. He pulled the goggles on and let them sit on his forehead. "Ready?"

"Ready," Astra said and downed her potion and pulled the goggles on, charging into the water.

Beneath the surface, the ground was fairly level for a few feet before abruptly dropping off into a deep abyss. Kicking deeper, Astra used one of her Summon Stones and called a water creature. The dolphin-like summon swam out of the summoning circle and stopped between her and Xander. Reaching out, she grasped the dolphin creature's fin. Xander did the same.

Soon, they were deep enough that light from the sun

barely glimmered through the murky currents. Her Water Sight goggles gave the structures beneath the lake a white outline-glow, revealing a sunken, destroyed city. They were near what used to be a tower. Several other towers lay on the lakebed, knocked over or collapsed from age. Their presence had been noticed. Something was coming. She cast Shelter on herself, Xander, and the dolphin, then looked around for the source of the aggro she could feel.

The lake monster came into view, its shape reminding her of a Liopleurodon. It rushed towards them with its great maw open. Speeding out of the way, the dolphin narrowly avoided getting its tail bitten off as the lake monster rushed past. Astra pulled her spear and stabbed the monster. The attack did damage but did not have the effect she'd wanted.

It came around for another attack. This time, Astra remained ready with her spear and as soon as the creature rushed past, she stabbed into the side of its jaw, getting the head of her spear caught. She released the dolphin and pulled herself flush with the lake monster's neck to keep from getting shaken off as it turned and twisted in the water.

Taking a sudden turn, the lake monster dove deeper, aiming for the tower she'd noticed earlier. Astra switched to daggers and dual wielding, using them to stab into the lake monster's skin and move around to the other side of its neck as it smashed itself into the rock, trying to scrape her off. The tower wobbled and collapsed. Her spear dislodged and drifted to the bottom, but Astra remained. This was going to take a while, she determined and glanced back to see Xander and her dolphin struggling to keep up.

On the bright side, Dual Wield and Blademaster had increased by a level.

"[Light]," Astra cast, aiming it at the horn on the end of the lake monster's nose. A blast of light exploded, as commanded.

Startled, the lake monster twisted in a circle.

"[Blemish]," Astra cast on the creature next aiming it into the wounds she'd caused with her daggers. The attack took hold, causing damage over time, but not enough for the monster to notice. "[Chaos]." This time, she aimed for the creature's eye, doing a minor amount of damage.

The monster turned, arching its side towards the debris on the lakebed. "[Tangle]," she cast. Vines sprang out of the city's remains, wrapping around the creature's head, but only briefly. It was enough to make it move away from the lake bottom and abort trying to scrape her off. "[Ice Flash]." She aimed for the horn on its nose again.

Mouth and nose freezing over, the lake monster turned in a circle once more, trying to flee whatever was attacking its face.

Astra kept on with the small attacks, working through multiple Skills she had no levels in yet to gain experience with them. Occasionally, she had to reposition, stabbing new holds into the lake monster's side and recasting Blemish. This would be a fight of attrition, but one the lake monster could not win. Astra had Xander following behind, ready to cast Cure on her any time she got even remotely close to getting hurt.

Rolling in the water, the lake monster had lost twenty-five percent of its health by the time it decided to try to retreat. Swimming hard for the rock wall where the shore abruptly dropped off, it dove into an underwater cave.

Seeing that she had no way of riding it through the hole, Astra pulled her knives free and kicked off, letting the lake monster go. Moments later, Xander caught up.

She pointed, indicating that they should follow.

Taking hold of the dolphin's fin, Astra hitched a ride into the dark cavern.

Two turns later and the area opened. The lake monster was still there, swimming in agitated circles.

"[Light]," she cast, frightening it further and keeping it going in the direction she wanted so it would be predictable. Ice Flash and Tangle became her other two monster herding spells.

It rounded on them for an attack. Astra blocked its mouth with an Ice Flash to the tongue, then blinded it with another Light spell. Thrashing, it hit the wall, breaking the ice out of its mouth. Xander grabbed Astra around the waist, dragging her out of the way as the monster's tail slapped where they'd been seconds before.

Astra remained unperturbed. She threw a Storm at the entrance of the cavern to keep the beast from escaping. She had to repeat the spell several times to discourage the monster from attempting to leave, even though casting electricity spells in water made the whole cave flicker to life with energy.

A fish floated past, belly up. It looked like something that would be useful later, so she grabbed it but didn't have time to stick it into her inventory, so it went into her physical pocket.

Fully enraged, the lake monster charged them again. Astra's dolphin dragged them in circles around the cavern.

Several level-up notices popped. Astra ignored them.

This battle was as tedious as the ones from the last few days, though it was taking much longer to take out the lake monster than mere Boars.

* * *

Xander had thought that five hours of water breathing would leave them plenty of time to kill multiple lake monsters.

Luckily, the cave they'd chased the lake monster into had air in it. They broke the surface, and Xander took several deep breaths before he dove again to grab the monster corpse and put it into his Inventory. Astra probably still didn't have any room in hers, despite giving away a bunch of stuff. By the time he got to the surface again, she'd climbed out onto a ledge and lay flat on her back.

"I'm exhausted," she said.

"I'm sure. That took longer than I thought it would."

"If I'd used my higher-level Skills, it might have gone faster... but I leveled everything I used to forty."

"Sounds like it was a fruitful endeavor anyway."

"Yeah. I've got a few more Mage Skills that could use that kind of treatment, but I need to get back to using the melee stuff." Astra turned her head to look at him. Her goggles had left marks around her eyes. She giggled at him.

"We'll find something big enough to give you a challenge like these creatures tomorrow. I think we've done enough leveling for today."

Astra propped herself onto her elbows. "This cave goes further back," she gestured. "We should check it out. I've got plenty of food in my inventory."

Xander glanced around. Indeed, the cavern seemed to have been made by sentient hands rather than natural. Admittedly, the people of Vard would worry, but... they could handle themselves for a day or two. He nodded to Astra. "After a short rest," he said.

She grinned and dropped back down. Lifting her hand, she swiped through the air, her eyes darting as she read something. Sitting up, she folded her legs and pulled some things from her Inventory. Moments later, she'd Crafted a spear, which she stuck back into her Inventory. She then Crafted several sets of leather armor and a few more weapons.

Last, she equipped some metal knuckle gloves. "I'm ready. Or wait. Lunch first." She pulled a pair of meals out of her Inventory, handing one to him.

Taking the plate, he took a moment to savor the scent before eating.

"You got the body of that Liopleurodon, right?"

"The what?"

Astra pointed at the water.

"Yes."

She nodded. "Probably has some good stuff in it. Is it me, or does this place look artificial?"

"It does," Xander agreed. "There are wheel ruts in the ground."

"Wonder if we'll find another lost city down here?"

"Perhaps." He thought for a moment. "To connect the two would be difficult, however."

"Lot of water between here and Vard," Astra said. "Unless whoever lives down here can swim." She looked at him with her head tipped. "Are there any mer-species on Ashguard?"

"Mer?"

"Fish people," Astra clarified.

"Not that I know of."

Again, she nodded, silently chewing for a moment. Her plate *poofed* as she finished the last bite. Moving to the water's edge, she washed her hands and face before sitting back on her feet, damp tail tapping behind her. Xander had to look away. She cut an impressive figure like that, and it was difficult to forget the other night when he'd gotten to see everything, regardless of what he'd said. He finished eating and washed up as well. Standing, he offered his hand down to her.

Astra looked up and took his hand, even though she didn't need it.

"Going with fists now?" Xander asked.

"Yep. Seemed easier, given the possible tight spaces we're going to be getting into."

Xander nodded and followed as she took the lead.

She started humming.

"It's been a while since I've heard that song," Xander mused.

"Oh?"

"It was one the bard frequently played at the Vanaheim Adventurer's Guild. It fell out of style some time ago." Admittedly, it was due to the Players leaving that the song lost popularity. The economy had crashed again, and much of the major cities were in ruins. Rightly, the people of Ashguard began to reject things the Players had introduced into the world, specifically music and fashion.

Astra's ears flicked down briefly. "It always makes me think of you," she admitted.

Xander smiled. "We did go to Vanaheim's Guild more often than the others," he recalled.

"Yeah. I noticed that you wandered off to talk to people whenever we went there, unlike the other Guild Halls. I thought it was kind of neat. Did you know a lot of people there? Tell me about them?"

"Mostly, I spoke with the other staff that took care of the Adventurer's Inn and Tavern. The other Porters I knew were rarely around."

"I wish whoever had made the game hadn't screwed things up so much," Astra said. "It would've been nice to talk to you all."

* * *

They'd been walking for hours, broken occasionally by fights with pale creatures that hadn't seen people in a thousand years. Astra could tell she was getting physically stronger with every battle and wondered if there were hidden character levels and not just Skill levels. Or if melee Skills imparted permanent stat boosts. If that were the case, how had Xander just been able to knife her that first day? Was she just that squishy without armor?

She glanced towards him in the strangely lit gloom of the tunnel. The ground remained flat and reasonably level with occasional lifts and dips, but it was apparent this had been made wide enough for two wagons to pass each other with clearance on either side. Luminescent fungi had been growing long enough to overflow the channels on the walls, mixing with the algae and other plants that thrived in low light.

"Do you smell any fresh air?" Xander asked.

"No," Astra said. "They did a good job with the flora to make sure there'd always be oxygen down here." She wandered closer to the wall to take a few samples of each to see if they could be used in Alchemy.

The only thing lacking was warmth. The place was exceedingly cold. Stuck in her uncomfortable armor, the exercise of walking wasn't quite enough to keep her warm. The occasional fights they got into with monsters worked up a sweat but left her sticky and freezing afterwards.

Ahead, she could see a different shade of gloom and squinted. "The path splits," she said. Jogging ahead, she found no signs of monsters nearby, so she investigated the neat corners of the path. If she'd not been convinced this was not a natural cavern, she was now.

"There's writing up there," Xander said. "I can't make it out; there are fungi on it."

Coming over, she squinted up at where he pointed. It was well above either of their heads. "Boost me," she said, "I'll wipe the stuff off."

Xander knelt, making a cup with his hands. Stepping in, she caught the wall when he easily lifted her to his shoulder height. She could just barely reach and quickly wiped the mushrooms and algae off, smearing bioluminescence around the carved lettering as she did so. "Nifelheim and Eldur," she reported.

She nearly lost her balance as he lowered her and

grabbed his head, her hands on his ears. Her foot slipped out of his hand, and he caught her in an embrace, one arm under her butt, the other on her back. Curious, she continued exploring his ears with her fingers, having not touched them before. He touched hers, it was only fair.

Until she saw his expression.

Xander's eyes had fallen closed, lips parted. His hand gripped her butt, pulling her tight against his chest.

His needy kiss sent shivers of pleasure through her and tingled in her breasts and between her legs. Xander knelt, placing her feet on the ground. He gripped her hair at the nape of her neck with one hand, holding her in place as he devoured her breath. Overbalanced, she helplessly toppled backward as he took them down to the floor. Crawling on top of her, his hands pulling at her armor, loosening the gorget to access her neck, which he nibbled and bit, his hand grasping at her breast despite the chest plate.

It was suddenly over when he came to his senses and sat back, face flushed. "I—forgive me..." he choked.

Astra stared up at him, mouth open in astonishment until it clicked. Grinning, she sat up. "You *naughty* man," she said. "You weren't sleeping with me because *I* needed it."

Caught in his lie, Xander dropped his head. The bioluminescence smeared on his ears, hair, and down his neck, made his blush even more prominent.

Shifting onto her knees, Astra grasped his hands, bringing them around her as she leaned in, claiming his lips.

Xander resisted at first, "I—"

"Shh. Just kiss me."

He pulled her into his lap, meeting her kisses with growing passion.

Astra slid her hands up his arms to touch his ears again. Xander moaned against her mouth and slipped his tongue in when she opened it to him. She felt a buckle loosen on her armor. "Xan—we stink..."

"I don't care. Jessica, please... I've kept my hands off you for so long. I can't wait anymore. Not when you touch me like that." Xander was breathless, completely undone by the heat of the moment.

She couldn't deny that she wanted him too.

Pulling her thighs around his hips, he ground himself against her, his hand pulling her hair. She could feel his heat despite the groin protection he wore. Abruptly, he sat back and tightened the buckles on her armor.

"You're right. We can't do this here," he said. He was flushed, panting for air. "Later. When we're somewhere safe, I'm going to..." He leaned down, claiming her mouth again. He couldn't finish his thought.

Astra wrapped her legs around him, pulling him flush to her. Despite the height difference when standing, he fit against her well, she thought. But he was right. They could get attacked at any time.

"Let's hurry back," she panted.

"Yes." Xander agreed but didn't immediately get up.

"I can teleport us," Astra offered.

"No."

* * *

Dawn was just starting to break when they got to Vard. The hunters were moving about, and Rita and White were likely at the kitchens. Astra started towards the bathhouse, but Xander stopped her, dragging her into their borrowed house instead.

Shutting the door quietly, he turned to face her.

"We're a mess," she said.

Opening his Inventory, Xander tossed the fur rugs she'd made on the floor, unequipped his armor, then grabbed her, wrapping her legs around him. "And we will be even more of a mess by the time I'm finished with you," Xander promised and kissed her. Laying her on the soft fur of the rug, he began unbuckling the straps of her gorget and shoulder pieces, tossing them aside. He could barely think, his dick was so hard. Xander just wanted to taste her. He wanted to put his hands on her plump breasts and squeeze.

She lay with her hands above her head, watching with those bright green eyes as he unwrapped her like a gift.

Pulling the leather breastplate off, he tossed it aside and slid his hands beneath the damp undershirt she wore, peeling it off her onyx skin. Bending down, he drew his tongue along her exposed flesh.

"Ah—" Astra gasped. "That tickles."

Tossing the sodden shirt aside, he grasped her breasts. Despite her petite frame, she overflowed his hands.

Her hands came up, sliding along his neck and against the long points of his ears. He couldn't help the moan and muffled it against her neck, kissing, biting gently. Reaching over his shoulders, she gathered his shirt in her hands and peeled it off over his head. Xander backed away to remove it entirely and laid down on her to feel her body, skin to skin.

His dick strained against his pants, pulsing with every heartbeat. He wanted inside her. He desperately needed inside her. Xander ground himself against her, feeling her hot core through her leather pants, the buckles of her leg armor biting into his skin as Astra pulled him against her. Finding her mouth, Xander kissed her softly, then hard.

Astra's nails scraped the damp skin of his shoulders as she returned his kisses. Drawing back for breath, she whispered his name, gaze unfocused even as she looked at his face.

Withdrawing, he sat back to start unbuckling her leg armor, pulling it off, and tossing them aside until he'd gotten down to her leather pants. Grasping them, he peeled them off, turning them inside out in the process.

Exposed, his black and white Felis lay with her knees apart, her white pubic hair a sharp contrast to her dark skin, her bedraggled tail twitching.

Xander went down, grasping her thighs as he put his mouth to her lower lips. Having dated a Felis before, Xander knew that hair in his mouth would be a thing he would have to deal with. Using his thumbs, he spread her labia, pushing her pubes aside to find her clitoris and gently suck upon it.

Astra gasped, her hands touching his hair, then gripping his head. Her tail twitched, flicking back and forth between his knees.

Sliding his fingers into her, Xander pressed upwards, gently rubbing.

Her thighs twitched, pressing against his ears. Her

fingers began to knead on his hair, pulling and scratching. Xander chuckled and dipped his tongue down to taste her juices. She whimpered. Her body tightened around his fingers as her hips moved involuntarily. Releasing her thigh with one hand, Xander pushed his pants down, releasing his throbbing erection. He was already wet with precum and didn't think he would last long once he got inside her.

She was absolutely dripping.

Moving his kisses up her body, he wiped her juices on the head of his cock, then slid himself inside.

Astra moaned, lifting her hips to meet him, then wrapped herself around as he filled her, drawing him in to kiss his mouth, her fingers fumbling at his ears.

To his surprise, she took him to the hilt, her core tightening around his cock as she ground her hips against him.

Grasping her breast with one hand, Xander began to thrust, feeling his orgasm building quickly. Her tail thumped against his thighs and knees, cold and wet. He thrust harder as her body began to shake. She clutched his shoulders, moaning into his ear as he pounded himself into her.

His cum filled her, and he sat back to grip her hips, pressing himself hard against her to urge every last drop from his body.

Her knees clamped tight; her body curled around him. Astra wiggled. "M-nomost..." she whimpered.

Drawing back, he began ramming her until she grasped his hands on her hips, digging her nails in, a look of ecstasy on her face.

Spent and exhausted, Xander dropped back to sit on his feet, falling halfway out of her. He shifted, pushing himself back in as he lay on top of her.

"I've wanted you for years," he whispered against her neck. "Every time you snuck into my blankets to lay with me... I wanted..."

She caressed his hair.

"I should've known you were awake..." she said.

Xander kissed her neck, then down to her collarbone. He could feel her tightening around him as her lust cooled, but he wasn't finished. He'd promised. He would deliver. Sitting back, he pulled his pants off the rest of the way and placed kisses upon her body.

Astra looked up at him in shock. "Again? So soon?"

"Yes," he told her, claiming her mouth for several long kisses. "This time, I will go slowly." He leaned in to whisper into her ear. "I want to hear you moan."

She shivered, a breath of excitement escaping her lungs.

* * *

Sticking their armor into her Inventory and getting dressed in their cold, filthy clothes, Astra couldn't help her deep flush as she did the Walk of Shame to the bathhouse. They'd gone at it four times. Loudly. It was full daylight now, and plenty of people were out and about now. She wasn't sure if she was imagining the knowing looks or not, but Xander didn't seem to care in the least. Did he have no shame?

Hurrying into the bathhouse, Astra sighed, shoulders

hunched, glad that it was empty.

"Was it bad?" Xander asked, sounding concerned as he came in behind her, ducking to get into the door.

"N-no!" Astra turned to look up at him. "I just... didn't want to advertise to everyone that... what we..."

Xander chuckled, his hand brushing along the top of her hair, then curled around her ear to gently tug. "They would find out no matter how secretive we were about it," he assured. He stripped his shirt off and dropped it into the communal laundry basket.

Astra stared at him. Bright red scratches adorned his porcelain skin down his shoulders, wrists, and hips. She hadn't even realized she'd done that.

"Come here," Xander said, touching her shoulder and sliding down to her hand, drawing her over to one of the spigots. "Let me help you wash." Xander had stripped her shirt before she knew what was happening, and he was completely naked again.

Still embarrassed, Astra pulled her pants off and tossed them into the laundry before getting a quick rinse so she could start soaping up. Xander started with her tail while she worked on her head. He was very gentle with it, working his way up from the tip to the base of her spine. Astra couldn't help but shiver at the sensation of him touching her there.

He pulled her back against him, breathing gently into her soapy ear as he asked, "Do you like that?"

Astra's knees shook slightly as he massaged the base of her spine. "Ah..." she breathed involuntarily.

"I'll take advantage of that," Xander said, tone absolutely wicked.

She turned her head to look up at him. "You... already knew that's a weak spot for Felis, didn't you?"

Xander smiled at her. That look he'd always had was on his face; the one she'd thought so was cold... Now she recognized it for what it was; barely contained lust.

She bit her lower lip. He would destroy her downstairs if she didn't set some boundaries now. "N-not in public," she said.

"As you wish," Xander said regretfully and released her breast and tail to start slathering soap up her back.

"Are you really still horny?" she asked.

Chuckling softly, Xander said, "I've been celibate for two hundred years."

"Man. Why?" she asked, soaping her front.

"Hm." He didn't want to answer, it seemed.

She looked over her shoulder at him, then turned to slather him in soap. "Fine, turn around."

He did so and took a seat on the bench so she could reach his hair. She tried her best to untangle it as she went.

They rinsed off together, dressed in fresh clothes, and returned to their bed.

Astra didn't get much choice as to whether they were naked again since Xander had stripped and dropped onto the bed as soon as the door was shut. Crawling over, she laid partially on his chest, one leg between his, her fingers caressing his skin.

His palms caressed her back.

"I should've died by now," she said.

"What do you mean?"

"My body, on Earth. I've been in Ashguard for how long now?"

Xander remained silent for a moment. "About a week," he said.

"Three days is long enough to die of dehydration, right?" she asked.

"More like ten," Xander said. "Is that what has been worrying you?"

"Yeah. I'm afraid... what's going to happen? Will I just disappear?"

He kissed her hair. "Astra... I think your body is already dead."

She pushed onto her elbows to look at his face.

"I felt you die five hundred years ago. You'd sent me to Aesir to sell things. It was midday, and your health dropped suddenly. I'd just turned to go to the Soul Stone when it felt as if..." Xander's hands tightened on her. "As if I'd been stabbed, the blade twisted and ripped out. I could still see your health bar at the corner of my vision. Empty." He cupped her face. "A presence that should have been there but would forever be gone. It took a long time to learn to ignore it."

Silence fell between them until she found the voice, the words, to ask her question. "Why didn't you say anything sooner?"

Xander shook his head. "It is a conclusion I've only recently come to. It is the only way your inability to leave would make sense." He cupped her shoulders. "This is your body now."

Astra lowered back down, placing her head on his chest as she stared into the void.

"I have also come to question whether Ashguard is real or not," Xander admitted. "The Skill system is far too convenient to have been something naturally occurring." He started stroking her ear.

"So, you think Ashguard is a game, and I'm dead, and my mind is stuck here," Astra concluded. "That's... a doozy."

Xander snorted. "An understatement," he mused. His fingers worked through her hair, gently scratching her scalp.

Astra's eyes slid closed.

The rumble that began in her chest startled her awake. "What was that?" she asked, sitting up slightly.

"You." Xander pulled her back down. "You purr in your sleep."

Astra stared into the distance as she tried to decide if she should be embarrassed about that or not.

"Another reason I like sleeping with you," Xander added, sounding barely awake now.

She settled further against his side and closed her eyes. It was apparently just something her new body did, she decided. Letting herself relax, she felt her purr begin again and let it.

* * *

"I tell you she's a liar," Glen said firmly, her voice echoing from the partially open sanctuary door as Xander approached. "She took our heirloom Skill Scrolls, and they've been wasted! She can't create anything of value for us."

"Says the one wearing robes she made," Ruth said.

"That's different," Glen said. "She disappeared

yesterday and has spent all day today in bed!"

"With me," Xander said, stepping into the sanctuary. His initial glance spotted piles of cloth, furs, wood, raw ore, and old tools pushed against the walls. He didn't have the opportunity to Examine them, though, since Glen's tail had puffed, ears back. "We went into the lake and killed one of the monsters there."

"Into the lake? For hours?" Glen demanded. "Impossible."

"Then what's the corpse I left outside?" he asked blandly and pushed the door open so the two women could see.

Glen gaped. Ruth just grinned. A crowd had gathered outside to look at the dead lake monster. One child was trying to climb the massive body.

"Ruth," Xander addressed, "We didn't get the chance to explore much of the submerged city. However, we did discover a tunnel that leads north towards Nifelheim. We only explored up to an intersection that branched towards Eldur before returning. I thought you should know about it."

"There were old stories that Vard had trading routes with Nifelheim through the mountains," Ruth mused, scratching her chin hair with her nails. "Were there monsters?"

"A few," Xander said and moved to the other side of the room to dump their corpses. "Not sure what their parts can be used for. Astra will be in shortly to look through everything. She was unloading the fish she killed at the kitchens."

"Fish?" Glen asked.

"Yes. When used as an area spell and cast in water, Storm kills lower creatures such as fish," Xander said blandly. "Astra collected them as it would be a waste not to."

Again, Ruth had to clear her throat instead of laugh.

"Xander! Why did you leave it out here?!" Astra objected as she approached. "Tearing it apart is gonna be messy as heck!" She came around the side and entered the sanctuary.

"Where would you like it instead?" Xander asked.

"Hnnf, I don't know. I want its blood too," Astra whined. "Just put it away for now?"

"As you wish," he said and brushed his hand against her cheek as he passed, a petty parting shot to Glen. He didn't bother looking to see her expression, though. That would have been a little too far.

Astra began reporting to Ruth and Glen on which Skills she leveled to fifty as she sorted through the materials piled in the sanctuary. "This is a lot of good stuff," she said. "I'll focus on Crafting the rest of today. We only got a few hours of sleep since getting back to town."

"Even though you spent all day in bed," Glen said sourly.

"We got back at nine this morning," Astra defended. "Then we needed to wash. It's only four now."

Xander glanced back now to see Astra facing Glen, her tail flicking in irritation.

"I just expected more dedication from you," Glen said coldly. "Not just fooling around."

"And what exactly does dedication look like to you?" Astra snapped. "I've leveled fifteen Skills in the last three days to fifty. I can only provide ten Scrolls a day. That's not a limit I set; it's just the limit."

"I expect you to be out training every day! Your mastery of any of the Skills I gave you have been poor!" Glen interrupted.

"You wanna fight me?" Astra asked. "Then let's fight! I'll bury you three times over before you can blink!"

Glen looked at Ruth. Ruth grinned. She was not going to stop this. Backed into a corner, Glen sneered, "You may have the Skills, but I have the mastery."

"Then to the beach," Ruth said. "So, everyone can see a demonstration of Astra's power."

Glen whirled away, head high as she stalked out.

The children who had been climbing on the lake monster corpse slid off and ran after. Taking that opportunity, Xander put the body back into his Inventory and waited for Astra and Ruth.

"I- I'm sorry, Ruth. I got carried away—"

"No, not at all," Ruth said and laughed. "Glen's been wanting this for a while, and since you," she pointed her stick at Xander, "have made your choice clear, she thinks one last show of strength will change your mind."

Xander shrugged. "She can think that."

Astra glowered and stalked ahead, sweeping her left hand to open her Inventory and equipped some armor. It was another set of mostly cloth with enchantments woven into it for elemental protection. It wasn't as good as the set that was currently in desperate need of cleaning, but it was still good.

Xander offered his hand to Ruth. "Would you like a lift down to the beach?" he asked.

"What a gentleman!" Ruth laughed and took his hand.

Carefully picking the old woman up, he carried her down the road faster than her old legs could take her. They arrived at the forest edge, and Xander set her down. "If everyone could gather closer to here, I'll ensure no stray spells hurt anyone." Once they had, Xander cast Shelter on the area and took a seat on the ground, looking forward to seeing Astra fight.

Taking place some distance down the beach from Glen, Astra flexed her fists.

Ruth stepped out. "Rules of engagement, ladies," she said. "Use only the Skills you got from Glen," she said to Astra. "Either yield or to the death. Your choice."

Glen gaped at Ruth, ears folding back.

"We have a very handsome—I mean, capable healer here who can revive you," Ruth said.

"I'll respawn at the Soul Stone if I die," Astra said. She was looking at something only she could see, then wiped the screen away.

"Ready. Fight!" Ruth shouted.

Astra's first shot was a Fire Bomb.

Glen countered with an Ice Flash, causing them to explode in steam, pelting the area with shards of broken ice.

However, Astra's actual attack had hit, lowering Glen's defenses with a Debuff.

"[Tangle]," Glen cast.

Unexpectedly, Astra cast [Fire Bomb] at her own feet, frying the Tangle instantly, and disappeared into the resulting smoke. Wind from the lake blew the smoke clear, but Glen hesitated. Astra was gone. She glanced at

Xander with a smirk, only to yelp when the ground began melting under her. A stone Golem rattled to life behind her and stood, slinging a stumpy fist at the back of the woman's head.

Glen landed face down in the mud but rolled over, shooting [Chaos] at the Golem.

It staggered, taking the spell in the chest, but it wasn't quite enough to bring it down.

The hair on the back of Xander's neck stood on end just before a bolt of lightning struck the ground next to Glen. Rolling away, the Mage got out of the [Quagmire] and away from the staggering Golem. Fury in her eyes, she drew her power to her hand and cast [Summon], bringing a fiery beast to life. She threw out her hand as her order to attack, and the Summon, resembling a burning bat, scrabbled across the rocks towards the blasted area Astra had been standing in before.

Astra's Illusion broke as the fire bat breathed a sustained blast of flames. Xander saw Astra's health take a hit, dropping ten percent, then twenty. She held out until the end, then countered with Debuff, Blemish, and Ice Flash in quick succession.

Taking the one-two-three to the face, the Hell Bat died, collapsing in on itself in charred ashes. Glen hadn't been standing and waiting, though. A ball of [Chaos] struck Astra in the chest, knocking her back several feet.

Rolling back up, Astra flicked out [Light], hitting the ground directly in front of Glen, followed by [Dark] just behind her. Glen flinched from the flash and staggered back into the sphere of darkness. Astra made another gesture, and Glen came flying out of the globe, landing hard on the stony beach. Astra's rock Golem stomped from the darkness after.

Fire Bomb exploded at Astra's feet. Her health dropped another fifteen percent. Xander laced his fingers together. He could not get involved until the fight was over.

Astra was on her feet again quickly. Glen took a moment to get up. Too long. The rock Golem caught up to her, grabbed her around the waist, and threw her to the ground.

Glen turned over and shot another [Chaos] at it, finally dismantling the spell and sending the loose, rattling stones back down to the ground where they belonged. She turned that hand on Astra and cast another [Chaos].

"[Debuff], [Blemish]," Astra called, throwing it on Glen. "[Death]."

Glen screamed in pain, writhing on the ground as she resisted the final spell.

Xander targeted her, finding that her health was nearly gone. One more hit, and she would die.

Ruth lifted her stick, shaking it. "Glen, do you yield?"

"No," Glen said through bloody lips as she climbed to her hands and knees.

"[Ice Flash]," Astra cast, freezing Glen to the ground. She struggled for a second before the Blemish took the last of her health and died. "[Cure]," she cast on herself and instantly returned to total health. "[Resurrect]," she hit Glen with it, leaving her still trapped in the Ice Flash.

Gasping, the woman blinked several times before realizing she was still stuck. "[Cure]," Astra cast, polishing off the last of Glen's health.

The mage sat there in silence, her gaze hollow.

Astra came to crouch in front of her, speaking softly for a moment before she stood and walked away.

"The winner is Astra," Ruth announced.

Removing her robes, Astra looked at Xander. "Out here would be fine to put that lake monster. There's plenty of space."

Xander got to his feet to move away from the crowd and dump the giant creature on the shore. When he looked back, Glen had gotten free of the Ice Flash and left the beach. Admittedly, she was powerful, but her lack of experience fighting other people was what had gotten her. Astra had fought against other Players a few times and had witnessed multiple other fights. There was no end to the dirty tricks one could pull, and if she'd had permission to use the full range of her Skills, the fight probably wouldn't have lasted half as long.

Drawing her hunting knife, Astra equipped a leather apron and started getting to work on taking apart the lake monster. Other hunters came to assist, and soon a massive slab of meat was on its way up to the kitchens.

* * *

Astra leaned back against the wall, legs stretched out in front of her as she watched the children playing in the snow.

Winter had been cold but pleasant, given that she had Xander to cuddle up with every night. She'd lost track of how many days she'd spent in Vard... in Ashguard, for that matter.

The leaves turned colors and fell to the ground. The

winter snow covered the mountains and iced the edges of the lake. In the last few weeks, the snow had begun to thaw. As time had passed and she'd not suddenly keeled over, she started to believe Xander's theory that she was already dead. After all, it was five hundred years after the last time she'd played.

Watching the seasons change in the mountains had been amazing. Back on Earth, the little town she'd lived in hadn't had much in the way of snow or trees. The seasons just went from hot and humid to cold and miserable. In the spring and fall, it flip-flopped on the daily, leading to extreme storms and hiding in the cellar.

Pulling her tail into her lap, she got a comb out of her Inventory to work on a snag she found.

Vard was as prepared as it was going to get. Everyone had new weapons and armor. Everyone had some level of Cure, Resurrect, and Regeneration. There were multiple people capable of Crafting at high levels, giving them the ability to make potions, items, and food that gave bonuses. All the Skills the villagers had given her were leveled up to fifty at least, and she'd given back at least one of each so the Skills could be taught the slow way to the children and wouldn't be lost.

Her relationship with Glen had never improved, though. The woman constantly glared at her. At least she'd quit hitting on Xander.

Speaking of Xander, she turned her head to look down the street as he approached.

She didn't know where he'd gone or what purpose, but Astra hadn't felt like getting up and moving after getting out of bed. He sat on the edge of the porch.

"Something bothering you?" he asked.

"I've been thinking. When is the Convergence supposed to come?"

Xander shook his head. "Soon. But I couldn't say with certainty. It is difficult to see the stars from here."

"Where would we go to be able to see them?" Astra asked.

"Nifelheim's Observatory," Xander said.

"Vard is as good as it will get," Astra said.

Xander nodded in agreement and moved to lean against the wall beside her. "We need to warn the rest of the world and help them prepare."

"I wanted to see if we could find Eldur, too," Astra said. "But checking on the Convergence is more important." Her ears flicked as a bug flew by. "We've got a choice... We could go quickly or slowly."

He nodded, bringing one knee up to prop his arm on it. "Announcing ourselves by using the Soul Stone or moving over land. It is a tough choice, given why we left in such a hurry to begin with."

"We're both much higher-level," Astra said. "We could take them."

"Killing them isn't an option. We need to convince them..."

"They want Skills, right?" Astra asked, rolling her head against the wall to look at him. "Then we'll give them Skills."

"They want unlocked Skills," Xander said.

Her ears folded briefly. "I don't know how that would work. I've never given a Skill to someone else's Porter. We'd have to test."

"We could consult the Nox Crystalis," Xander suggested.

"I don't know what that is," Astra admitted.

"It is in the Church of Terra."

Astra scratched her neck absently. "Two reasons to go to Nifelheim next."

"We could compromise," Xander suggested. "Follow that tunnel towards Nifelheim and see how far it goes. If we get blocked, we can teleport in through the Soul Stone. Coming in through the tunnel would allow us to enter the city quietly and see what has been happening before announcing ourselves. I also know someone in the Lower City who might be willing to assist us with testing."

She smiled at him, lifting her hand to caress his cheek. "Okay. Sounds like a plan. When do we leave?"

"Once you feel like we've got enough supplies to last for a few months on the road," Xander said, turning his face towards her hand to kiss her palm.

"Okay. We should go hunting then. I don't want to take supplies from Vard after all we did to help them beef up their reserves." Astra pushed off the wall and slid to the edge of the porch.

www.ingramcontent.com/pod-product-compliance
Lightning Source LLC
Chambersburg PA
CBHW070928250626
47159CB00009B/3165

www.ingramcontent.com/pod-product-compliance
Lightning Source LLC
Chambersburg PA
CBHW060848250626
47159CB00013B/2765